Garbage Night
at the *Opera*

Garbage Night
at the *Opera*
stories

Valerie Fioravanti

Winner of the G.S. Sharat Chandra Prize for
Short Fiction selected by Jacquelyn Mitchard

 BkMk Press
Universtiy of Missouri-Kansas City

BkMk Press
University of Missouri-Kansas City
5101 Rockhill Road
Kansas City, Missouri 64110
(816) 235-2558
www.umkc.edu/bkmk

Financial assistance for this project has been provided by the
Missouri Arts Council, a state agency.

Executive Editor: Robert Stewart
Managing Editor: Ben Furnish
Assistant Managing Editor: Susan L. Schurman
Editorial assistant: Linda D. Brennaman
Cover art/design: Matthew Maxwell

The G. S. Sharat Chandra Prize for Short Fiction wishes to thank Naomi
Benaron, Leslie Koffler, Linda Rodriguez, Brian Shawver.

BkMk Press wishes to thank Claire Brankin, Elizabeth Gromling,
Ben Hlavacek, Paul Tosh, Anna Monardo, Gregory Van Winkle,
Brandi Handley, Marie McKim Mayhugh.

Library of Congress Cataloging-in-Publication Data

Fioravanti, Valerie.
  Garbage night at the opera : stories / Valerie Fioravanti.
     p. cm.
  ISBN 978-1-886157-84-2 (pbk. : alk. paper)
  I. Title.
  PS3606.I66G37 2012
  813'.6--dc23
                                    2012033704

Printing by Versa Press, Inc.
This book is set in Candara, Myriad Pro, Bickham.

In memory of my mother and her family,
and their love for a worn-out neighborhood
they called the garden spot.

Acknowledgments

Some stories first appeared, in different versions and/or under different titles, in the following publications: "Garbage Night at the Opera" and "Earning Money All Her Own" in *North American Review*; "Kissing Decisions" in *Night Train*; "Beer Money" in *Harpur Palate*; "Local Man" in *REAL*; "Mama Loves You" in *Cantaraville*; "Weeds" as "Why I Hate Geraniums" in *Baltimore Review*; "Seventeen" in *Hunger Mountain*; and "Bouquet" in *Green Mountains Review*.

I'd like to thank my teachers: Hayes B. Jacobs from the New School; Marcia Golub, Joshua Henkin, and Kaylie Jones from the Writer's Voice program; and Kevin McIlvoy, Robert Boswell, Antonya Nelson, and Connie Voisine from New Mexico State University. Ali Tufel, for being my first writing mentor/friend. Kate Brentzel, for reading my earliest words. Philip Welsh, for urging me to "get out of my own way." Dorine Jennette, for telling me, "this was a manuscript, now it's a book." My editors Ben Furnish and Susan Schurman. Ana Cotham, Tatiana Morfas, and Jennifer Langdon for making Sacramento such a great place for this writer to live.

Garbage Night
at the *Opera*

Foreword

These stories charm, illuminate and intrigue. They provoke the heart and comfort the mind, and display the generosity and wisdom characteristic of the best of short fiction. Long after turning the last page, the reader is part of the texture of these worlds, rocked in the fabric of the writer's vision.

Jacquelyn Mitchard
Final judge
G. S. Sharat Chandra Prize for Short Fiction
author of *The Deep End of the Ocean* and *Second Nature: A Love Story*

Garbage Night at the $\mathcal{O}$pera

$\mathcal{L}$*a Bohème.* A thing of beauty, sung in his own language, the soprano his own countrywoman. A taste of home. *Cinque dollari* for tickets for students. A treat for his Franca, who doesn't know her heritage, has too little music in her life. Massimo would change that today at the matinée l'Opéra Metropolitan, across the river, in Manhattan. They would listen to the beauty, take in the sadness that is still beautiful, cry for the woman dying on the stage, her last breath a song for love. Together they would cry for Elena—his wife, Franca's mother—and feel their grief a little lighter for this beauty that is also sadness. After the music ends and the curtain falls, there would still be some light left before dusk. It wouldn't be too late for the subway ride home, for his mother-in-law to worry about Franca's bedtime, her safety as they walk home after dark, past the people who roam outside the neighborhood at night, with their cold, unflinching eyes.

Massimo clips the advertisement from *Oggi*, the Italian newspaper, as proof of the small price for students. He fears it is a misprint, but if he brings the clipping along it must be honored. He has learned this much in his years here, the attitude so different from home, where such mistakes are laughed at and accepted. He puts the clipping in his wallet, along with his photo card from the community college. He takes bookkeeping there three afternoons a week, a work program for single parents the employment counselor found for him. Massimo is the only father in the class. He is good with his figures, although he struggles sometimes to understand the quick words of his teachers. He hopes another business will open soon where the cardboard factory closed, or anywhere along the docks where almost all the buildings stand empty. He is not the only father out of work.

Massimo must also prove Franca is a student. He thinks it should be obvious, but like at home, *documenti* are important here. He sits with the firebox open in his lap, but he hesitates to remove Franca's birth certificate, fearing his wife would not approve. He shuffles the other papers, and chooses Franca's latest report card from her second-grade teacher. He prays to Saint Cecilia, the patron saint of music, that he has everything he needs to get them in. He wants Franca to have this chance to hear the music live, instead of the scratchy recordings he listens to only in the basement, exiled—by the ears of the other tenants who don't know music—to where the hum of the laundry machine drones day and night.

He pulls his suit from the closet, and the mothball scent clings to the plastic covering. He has not worn it in the last fourteen months. He holds it to his chest, tucks in his head and squeezes his large frame through the kitchen window, onto the fire escape where it can be aired. As soon as he unzips the garment bag, the memories of his wife's funeral escape like trapped moths. He ducks from them, focuses on the tasks to be done.

His suit sways roughly as he irons Franca's white blouse. He does this with the flat of his ironing board propped across the fire-escape railing. His kitchen windows face another building, and the light that filters in is dim. Massimo hates to live by the lamp during daytime, so he works outside, making the shaky, bathtub-sized fire escape into a balcony where he can absorb whatever brightness the stingy skyline allows.

His view as he irons is brick painted tan to resemble the more durable brownstones of other neighborhoods. Massimo believes this trick fools no one. He has lived with this horizon for ten years, and the paint has always been peeling, with the specks of red peeking through accentuated by brown streaks creeping from rusty drainpipes on the roof. In Camogli, his village, their homes were painted in shimmering golds and reds with unique border designs and contrasting shutters, mostly green. Massimo cannot duplicate the light of his homeland, but he has tried to beautify his fire escape by running a creeping vine to introduce some color. The firemen brought ladders and chopped it away with their axes. They said it was a safety violation, wrote him a ticket, and warned him not to do it again.

He still has his flowers, which he coaxes to life in pots and boxes, but they have to be kept inside at night so they can't be used as target practice (this, apparently, violates no code worth enforcing). Each time he forgets and has to sweep up the broken shards and blossoms he comes closer to giving up, not replanting, scattering all his remaining seeds in the wind. He fears the probability of this day, the *if* slowly becoming *when*, like the slow drip of water eroding stone.

Franca pokes her head outside, lets him know she is home from her grandparents, who have an apartment two floors below them. Franca doesn't like the fire escape: her feet are small enough to slip through its iron slats when she isn't careful, and it trembles when the subway runs below their street. She doesn't mind the lights running all day long, doesn't long to be outside all the time the way he does, although she usually likes being wherever he is.

He passes her white blouse through the window, tells her they are going to the opera. "Nana's doing wash now," she says.

"We're going into the city to see *La Bohème.*"

"Oh," she says, turns from the window, changes her mind, turns back. "Do I have to take another bath?"

He finishes her pleated skirt and passes it through the window also. "No time," he says, with a sigh. He motions her away from the window and props the ironing board against the stove. Coming back inside is always harder for him, when he has to shimmy through the window, bring his feet down where he can't see. It is yet another thing he can't get used to.

He changes into his suit and buffs his shoes a final time as he waits for her to be ready. She comes out in her robe, her white tights and black patent shoes visible, holding something wrapped in plastic high above her head. "Can I wear this instead?"

It is a blue jumper her aunt had sent for her birthday, too big and then forgotten when her mom entered the hospital for the final time. Massimo puts the hanger around Franca's neck to check the fit, which seems right. "Try it on."

The dress is still a bit large, but Franca prances around, obviously pleased. The color reminds him of his sister's letters, how she writes about the sky in Arizona, which she claims on a clear day goes on in all directions, larger than the whole of Europe. He knows she must exaggerate, but he would like to see it with his own eyes one day, introduce Franca to her Aunt Luisa. He used to hope to join her, help with the restaurant she still dreams of opening. His wife refused to leave her parents and her home, a point it was hard for him to argue against. Now even the letters postmarked *Tucson, AZ*, fill his mother-in-law's eyes with tears, but he can't ask Franca to leave her Nana or willingly cause his wife's mother that much pain. Franca doesn't spend much time looking at the sky.

He fixes her collar, which is tangled in the straps of the jumper, and they leave. They walk the four blocks to the subway entrance, Franca's hand securely within his, her body tucked safely in the shadow of his left side. The train comes quickly, and an elderly woman slowly makes room for Franca on the bench. Massimo stands beside her, hums the overture in anticipation, which makes Franca smile and try to follow along. They transfer two more times before climbing their way above ground, across the street from Lincoln Center.

They pass a row of banners advertising performances: ballet, orchestra, chamber music, theatre, opera, even movies, each specialty with its own hall or stage or screening room. The complex is built to resemble a European town square, but as grand as the fountain in the center or the tall arching windows may be, it all seems too shiny, lacks the weathered grace of what it is meant to imitate. Even as he passes judgment, Massimo is grateful to be here, and he urges his daughter forward as she stops and starts, trying to take in all that she sees.

There is no line at the ticket counter, which is a little wooden booth with a glass window, leaving only enough of an opening for money to be exchanged. The microphone the clerk speaks into eats her words, delivers only squeaks and static. Massimo points to Franca. "Two tickets for students, please."

More squeaks. Massimo slides his documents and ten dollars under the glass. The woman pushes it back to him, squeaks some more. Massimo points to his ear, walks around the side by the booth door. He has to knock twice before she opens it a crack and says, "Show's sold out."

Massimo shoves his foot in the crack before she can close the door again. "Please, I can make fix for you, for two tickets." He tries to hand her the clipping, but she won't take it. "The inside is dirty, it needs to be cleaned."

"It's not dirty in here," she says, tries to pull the door shut with his foot still in it. "Get away from here before I call security."

"He means the microphone," Franca says impatiently. Massimo's eyes shift to the floor, which looks like the marble of Carrara, a town only a few hours from his own. He doesn't like it when his daughter speaks for him, but strangers often misunderstand him. As young as she is, Franca has learned to adopt a certain tone, a sharpness that implies the fault is with the listener. To Massimo, this is a very American quality, although her mother, also born here, did not possess such surety. "My father is offering to fix it for you if you sell us the tickets to *La Bohème*. He can fix anything. Everyone who knows him says so."

The woman seems charmed by Franca, lifts the edges of her mouth with some effort. "There are no tickets, sweet thing, the entire run is sold out. I can't help you, and I can't let anyone who isn't union touch any of the equipment here, no matter how useless it is." A buzzer goes off, and the woman jerks her head back inside the booth. "I have to help these people." She leaves Massimo with his foot still jammed in the door.

Massimo hands the clipping to Franca. She reads it and shrugs, repeats what the woman told them, but he doesn't want to believe there are no more tickets. He pokes his head into the booth and sees the woman handing an envelope through the slot. "Those are tickets, no?" he says.

The woman jumps from her stool, points her finger at Massimo. "Look here Mister, you have to get outside right now."

Massimo backs out of the booth, but still plants his foot in front of the door. "We stand," he says.

"That couple paid for those tickets months ago, with a credit card. All the tickets are long gone, and there's no standing allowed."

"He really loves the opera," Franca says.

"No, for my daughter." Massimo puts his hands on Franca's shoulders. "I want her to see. Don't make me disappoint her."

"I can't help you. Why don't you take her to the park? There's an entrance straight down 66th Street, and it's safe. You shouldn't stay after dark, but it's safe now." She reaches back for her purse and rifles through it, pulling out a pack of lifesavers. She peels back the wrapper, popping two greens in her mouth before she hands Franca the cherry one. She offers the roll to Massimo but he shakes his head, pinches Franca, who says "Thank you" on command. He pulls his foot from the door, his shoulders slumping as he turns away.

"Kids love the park, Mister. My husband takes the grandkid there all the time. There's this puppet show by the fountain, before you go down the steps. That's all he talks about for hours after he sees it, every time."

"*Grazie,*" Massimo mumbles and leaves. Franca follows, taking his hand.

"The park sounds nice, too. We can listen to your records when we get home. I'll do my phonics homework downstairs with you."

Massimo smiles clownishly and swings her arm in jump-rope

arcs as they walk. He can see the anxiety melt from her step, the tightness behind her eyes begin to fade. The last thing he needs is to see his failures cause her worry, trigger an impulse to make him happy at any cost. That is not a thing for children to do, and Massimo's chest pinches at the thought of her carrying so many adult burdens. They cross Broadway, and Massimo asks a policeman standing by the corner about the park. His wife's parents sailed to America, found an apartment in Brooklyn, and rarely strayed more than a few streets beyond their home. Both their children lived on the same street after they married. His wife had once been angry with him for more than a week for taking Franca to the Botanical Gardens by bus, to see the cherry blossoms in bloom. He still doesn't understand why that was so dangerous, but it is harder now to go against her wishes when she can't argue back. The *polizia* assures him it is safe, agrees that the puppet show is worth seeing, and gives them directions to the fountain. Massimo thanks him and takes Franca there to try and salvage their day.

The puppets, when they find them, are five marionettes that dance to blues music and pretend to sing along to the soundtrack playing from a boom box, their shaggy hair and loose limbs flopping to the beat. Franca watches them cycle through their act, three songs of about three minutes each—with time in between to pass the tip basket through the audience—for over an hour. She says it's like watching *The Muppets* without a television, but to Massimo it is the poorest of substitutes. It sickens him to watch, knowing his own child is pleased. He looks at his watch and tries to imagine what they would be seeing if they had their tickets to *La Bohème*. He places himself in the poor Paris apartment, with the artists burning pages for the fire, imagines Franca's growing excitement as she watches the performers, cranes her neck to see the musicians playing in the pit below the stage. Massimo is humming "*Questo Mar Rosso*" when the tip basket presses into his ribs. When he ignores the man with the basket, he is serenaded with an a cappella version of "Stand by Me" until he parts with two quarters.

To pass the time, Massimo chats with a man in a brown uniform, a park ranger from the patch on his sleeve, but all he knows of rangers is the hockey team. Ranger Steve is from Yugoslavia, a country only a ferry ride away from his own. He is also from the coast, and they begin to talk about the sea and the light they miss from home. *Stafan* has never been to the opera, but he likes his job caring for the park. Massimo says it is the largest bit of green he's seen in America, and this surprises his new friend. Massimo confides that New York was supposed to be a pit stop on his way west. Stafan reveals he has three young sons in New Jersey, and a cousin on a ranch in Montana he still dreams of joining.

Stafan guides them to the zoo on the park's east side, but they detour for a ride on the carousel they spy sitting on a hill in the distance. Franca rides a wooden horse with a golden saddle, its reddish-brown coat painted the same shade as her mother's hair. After, when they are searching for the path to the zoo, two women trot by on horseback. Franca's energy stills as she watches the horses long after they fade from Massimo's view. It's as if she never quite believed in them as real, breathing creatures.

The zoo's main attraction is a polar bear, and his lair is set up so you can view him from different heights and angles, both above and below the water. He is a beautiful creature, swimming from end to end, his white fur shimmering in silver streaks as he glides through an easy breaststroke. The viewing area is well placed in the corner where the polar bear makes his turn, pushing off the glass with a hind paw larger than Massimo's head. This occurs at eye-level, and Massimo watches the tendons in his leg flex and strain, as the glass vibrates and then slowly absorbs the shock. He picks up Franca, so she can get a closer view, and together they watch the polar bear swim toward them, twist his trunk, and push off against the glass over and over and over again. They notice the black pads of his paws in contrast to his white fur, the shades of silver and charcoal as the muscles ripple his fur, revealing the under-layers protected from the water.

Franca's nose presses against the glass as she watches, turning away only if she has a new wonder to share. Massimo has a

crick in his neck from holding her so long. He stretches his muscles, and as he looks up he sees two men tossing a beach ball back
and forth across the water, and a third dangling a long stick with
a large fish speared at the end into the water as the polar bear
passes by. Massimo watches the rebellion of the polar bear, his
refusal to take the food they offer if he will stop swimming his
laps and play. The man with the stick becomes insistent, bringing
the pointed end closer and closer to the polar bear, who does not
stray from the lane his habitual swimming has created, and thus
allows himself to be poked. Massimo can watch no longer. He
puts Franca down and tugs her away against her will. "I want to
see more," she says.

"No," he says, and points out the three men, but Franca twists
away and runs back to the tank. Massimo lets her go.

She joins him a few minutes later, takes his hand. "It's not the
same now."

They walk north, toward the French garden at the very edge
of the park—as if the French didn't learn this from watching Italian things grow—but the sun is starting to set, and even Stafan
warned him to leave the park before dark. Massimo has trouble
finding a path that will take them out of the park, because they all
seem to loop back to where they started. He sees a couple in the
distance, walking arm in arm, and cuts through the trees to follow
them.

By the time they exit, near the Guggenheim Museum, it is
now dark and they are on the opposite side of the park from
where they started. From his subway map, Massimo knows
the line runs along Lexington Avenue, but he's not exactly sure
where that is. He knows Lexington Avenue is east, so he crosses
the street and walks away from the Park, trying to mask any con-
fusion he feels. After crossing Madison, he sees an old dresser
by the side of the curb. The finish is stained, but the carvings are
fine. He knocks along the sides and inspects the drawers, but
the dresser has only cosmetic flaws. He's pretty sure it's made
of mahogany, and if so, he might be able to fix it up and sell it

for enough money to cover two tickets to the opera, paid for in advance.

He picks it up, and although it is weighty, he can carry it. He puts it back down and walks partway up the street to read the sign. Park is next, not Lexington. Franca hops over the cracks in the sidewalk, mumbling a jump-rope song. Until he knows exactly where they are, he must focus on getting her home safely. He leaves the dresser behind, but Lexington is the next block after Park, and when he turns the corner, he can see the green subway lollipops glowing up ahead. He goes back for the dresser, already sketching out plans for the work, debating which opera to choose.

They walk back toward the subway, but his pace slows. Franca skips along ahead of him, doubling back whenever he whistles that she's too far ahead. When Massimo loses sight of her and she doesn't come quickly back into view, he hitches the dresser a little higher and picks up his pace. When he sees her, she is eyeing a bicycle being brought to the curb. She waits until the man sets the bike down by his trash bins and bundled newspapers, then runs over to it as soon as he turns away.

"Don't touch that, it's broken."

Franca circles the bike. Three spokes jut out around a dent in the rim, but the rest of it, purple with a white basket embossed with flowers, white and purple streamers sprouting from the handlebars, seems fine. "It's just the wheel, right?" she asks.

"Won't work without the wheel."

"My father can fix it for me." Franca points to Massimo, and he nods. He holds the dresser in his arms.

The man says nothing.

"Is it okay if I take it?"

The man looks at Massimo, then back to Franca, but remains silent.

"I don't have a bicycle, and my father could make this one work for me."

"It's not too hard to make fix," Massimo says. "It would be a shame for it to waste."

The man looks back toward his building, which has high steps and a door with a stained-glass window, as if searching for guidance. Franca looks along with him. "You can take it, I guess."

"Can you handle it?" Massimo asks.

Franca's body bobs *yes*. She grips the handlebars and jerks the bike into the air. It knocks her over and falls back where it began. Massimo sets the dresser down and helps her to her feet. He places his foot between her legs and nudges them further apart, so her feet align with her shoulders. He bends his knees slightly and gestures for her to do the same. Massimo picks the bike up and places her left hand on the bar beneath the seat. Franca says, "I'm ready."

"You can't expect her to carry that." The man pulls the handlebars from her grip, setting the colorful streamers in motion. Franca jumps back, startled by his sudden motion. "She's just a little kid—it's inhuman."

Massimo glances at the dresser, thinks of the opera money, and sighs heavily. He hooks the bicycle under one arm, and takes hold of Franca's hand.

"I can carry it. I don't want you to leave the dresser."

"You can't leave that piece of junk on my property."

Massimo puts the bike down and moves the dresser over by one building.

"You don't live there either. Maybe you need to take your garbage with you and leave mine alone."

Massimo steps closer to this pinched man who protects his discards like a vulture. His arm cocks and his fingers curl under his thumb. The man steps back as Massimo plows forward. Massimo is not a tall man, but he is large in the shoulders and chest. Franca hoists the bike on its hind wheel and rolls it between her father and the man. "Look, I can wheel it this way." She smiles with her whole face. "We just live two blocks away, mister. Please let me take it, please."

"You live two blocks away from here?" the man asks, his voice cracking on away.

Massimo uncurls his fingers, stares into the hand that made the fist. He is a man who hates violence. When he doesn't answer, the man says, "I think I'm going to keep the bike."

Franca spins the bike toward the man and lets go. Massimo picks her up and puts her safely behind him as the bike skids across the cement. "You threw it away," she says, lunging out from behind her father.

Massimo points in the direction they came from. "We live that way. We moved because her mother died. She has no mother and she has no bike."

The man blinks, looks everywhere but into Massimo's eyes. "You can take it," he says and walks quickly away, inside.

"*Grazie*," Massimo calls out, although he wishes he could leave the bike where it is. Franca circles around her father, showing him she can handle the bike on her own. He takes a closer look, and the bike is sturdy and well made. They have both chosen well.

They walk to the subway entrance. Massimo puts the dresser down at the top of the subway steps, but Franca picks the bike up carefully, bending at the knees, her legs firmly planted. "I can do it."

Massimo watches her take two careful steps down. She turns her head, says, "I want to do it myself," just as he is about to take the bike from her. She fights for solid footing as he prays for the courage to stand and watch. She sets the bike down after clearing the seventh and final step and dances around, her arms raised in victory. She looks up at him, and her eyes, a swirl of his brown and her mother's green, explode with light.

Kissing *Decisions*

*N*ikki's Uncle Pete was sprawled across the hood of an old Chevy parked in front of the bar, bullshitting with another half-dozen men taking a breather from their barstools. She tugged her shorts down to cover more leg, but felt a thin band of air hit her waist. She stamped her foot, then froze. It was worse when she moved too freely. Nikki needed her own clothes instead of hand-me-downs, but her mother didn't see the harm in baring a little thigh or midriff. She said, "It's never too soon to show off a figure like yours," when Nikki complained.

"Let's cross," Nikki told her cousin.

"He's my Dad, you shit," Rae said.

"It's not a skeevefest for you."

Rae replied with an emphatic double finger.

Uncle Pete slid off the car. His shirt reflected the blue neon Pabst sign in the window. The corner reeked of ground-in beer and urine, the sidewalk layers as revealing as tree rings: *proudly serving our fourth generation.* "Baby girl, keep walking if your Mama sent you down here."

"Nothing wrong with her lungs," Rae told him.

Uncle Pete planted a yeasty kiss on Rae and then Nikki. "You two sneaking off to meet boys?"

Nikki gasped, and Rae kicked her. "Just playing handball with Mikey and Tim."

"*Hand*ball," some drunk said. "I'd sure like me a game of that." Nikki didn't look too hard to place him. He was bound to be somebody's uncle or brother. It was better not to know.

*Hand*ball Man took an elbow to the head from her cousin Tommy. "Show some respect." Tommy caught his sister Rae by the waist and spun her, spilling beer from his bottle in an impressively round circle.

"That is one sweet, juicy apple offa Grace's tree." Nikki looked away, tried not to connect the voice to her friend Karen's father. That sucking-teeth sound was bad enough from the boys. It gave her gooseflesh on the inside when the old men tried it.

"Watch that talk," Uncle Pete said. "Girl's just fourteen."

"She's twelve!" Rae swatted her father, enough to set him stumbling into Tommy. "*I'm* older."

Uncle Pete squeezed Rae's cheeks in retaliation. "Sorry, baby. It's easy to forget."

Tommy grabbed Nikki by the neck and messed up her hair. "Nope, still pretty."

Rae's hands balled into fists. "Come on already!"

Nikki followed behind her as she kicked at every piece of trash in sight. "Told you we should've crossed."

"I don't see why they've always got to be looking at you." Rae whizzed a juice bottle her way, and it shattered between them, adding new shards to the already glittering street.

"Ask Mikey."

Rae attacked the curb with both feet. "I'm sick of hearing him say your name!"

Nikki climbed onto the mailbox and waited for Rae's tantrum to end. "Just kiss him yourself."

Rae played balance beam with the curb, moving too quickly for control. "My mom says you have to play love smart."

Nikki didn't see why she had to be a part of Rae's love game with Mikey. The mailbox bolts were loose, so she rocked it, taking comfort in the motion. "Don't make me do this."

Rae pulled her off the box. "Let's go, we're late."

Mikey leaned up against the wall of the old cardboard factory, cigarette in one hand and a beer in the other. His dark lashes rimmed the lightest green eyes, but Nikki figured he'd join the crowd at the bar sooner than most. Nikki couldn't understand why Rae didn't see this. It made love seem dumb, not blind.

"Tell him to go home and brush his teeth."

"I brought a pack of breath mints," Rae said.

"Don't let him stop at one."

"Don't be such a princess." Rae skipped off to meet Mikey.

Tim waved his ball in greeting, then slapped some hard shots against the wall. The old cardboard factory was their main court, although nobody played after dark. The block-long walls were full of private nooks and quiet corners.

"We're not here to play, moron," Rae said.

"Really?" Tim pointed at himself and then Rae. "What are we supposed to do?"

Nikki laughed as Rae launched another double finger. Tim was an easy boy to like, and Nikki didn't mind his dark red hair at all. What they said about red-haired boys just wasn't true. Nikki knew Tim wasn't a fag. She caught him looking all the time, whenever Mikey's attention was somewhere else. If Mikey would just turn in the right direction, they could all be kissing.

"I'll play a quick game with you." Tim's smile never made her feel dirty.

"Go stand over there," Rae commanded. Tim looked away, and Nikki baby-stepped into position.

Rae had her hands on Mikey's shoulders, and his head bobbed as she talked. Nikki didn't understand why someone as bossy as Rae couldn't tell Mikey that she'd be handling the kissing, now and in the future.

Rae nodded her way, and Nikki leaned against the wall and looked in Mikey's direction just as she'd been coached. Mikey swaggered forward, chest puffed out and arms swinging goonishly. When they were nose-to-nose, she laughed, her reluctance finally bursting from its cage. Mikey froze long enough for Nikki to see his eyes water. When he sped off toward the far side of the factory, Rae followed.

Rae had warned her not to mess up, but that probably meant she would ignore Nikki for a while. A break from Rae was like a vacation from noise.

"You can't ever do to that to a guy." Tim's ball punctuated each word. "Mikey *really* likes you."

Nikki was tired of feelings being so important when nobody much cared about her own. Tim pushed her up against the wall, his own macho showing as his ball slowly bounced away. "He likes me now," she said. "You've always liked me."

Tim's bangs fell in his face as he tried to avoid her eyes. Nikki swept them back into place, and her fingers buzzed from the contact. "I like your hair."

Tim's hands slid from her shoulders to her waist, and she shifted her hips from the wall as his arms reached around her. He checked behind him for signs of Mikey or Rae, and his whole body quivered as his lips touched hers. When his mouth opened it was warm, and his tongue was slow and gentle. Gradually Nikki slid down the wall with him, but he broke away when they heard Mikey and Rae skipping trash can covers down the street.

"It'll be worse than just Mikey," Tim croaked. "Every day I'll get pounded."

Nikki nodded. Tim wasn't the boy the other kids feared. He was the boy who helped pick up your books once his friends were done tormenting you. He wasn't the boy who was allowed to get the girl.

Tim pulled her to her feet. "You know those books you hide behind fashion magazines?"

"Like you hide science magazines behind comics?"

Tim tucked her hair behind her ears, then thrust his hands deep into his pockets. "You don't need to pretend. Smile some more, and they won't mind you're a little bit different."

"Smiling is pretending."

"Your life is so hard." Tim's lips curled, but he didn't smile. Nikki could tell it was a struggle.

"You know, I've heard that subway thing actually leaves the neighborhood. Two people could get on and meet up somewhere safe."

Tim's cheeks flushed as dark as his hair, and he couldn't hide his teeth any longer. "Smart chicks are hot."

Nikki's cheeks matched his, but they could hear Rae and Mikey trash-talking. Tim chased down his ball as Nikki held up the wall. Mikey approached more cautiously this time, and Rae raised her fist in warning.

Mikey kissed like he walked, all hard swagger. Nikki opened her mouth, but she couldn't bring herself to move her tongue. Mikey used his own tongue more forcefully, shifted positions roughly, pressed harder against her body. Always more of something, never less. Eventually he stopped. Nikki remained silent, and he nodded as if he finally understood.

On the way home, Nikki said, "In the future, all my kissing decisions will be my own."

Rae jumped in place, her full-body version of a nod. "Mikey got to be your first."

"No one will ever say he wasn't."

Rae stopped. "What does that mean?"

"Not everyone is showy and loud."

Rae raced ahead and slapped the stop sign three times, proving she was proud to be loud. "One day soon they're *all* going to notice what a freak you are."

An hour ago Nikki would have shivered and backed down. Instead, her mouth curled upward, slowly but not unnaturally.

Earning Money All Her Own

The afternoon Brooklyn Box & Paper announced they would shut down and terminate nearly four hundred workers (five of them members of her family), Angela Grotto's paycheck was hers to spend as she pleased.

She spent her lunch hour in the bank line, her passbook securely in hand as she waited her turn. Angela had four sisters: three older, one younger, all married. Not one of them had a savings account in her own name, money hers and hers alone to spend, not even Alma who had worked part-time at the parish rectory for ten years before she married at thirty-two, the same age Angela was now. Everyone Angela knew believed it was a shame that she was still single, but Angela had seen enough of married life not to mind so much herself.

When Angela reached the window, she instructed the teller, Mary Francis (her brother Paulie's first girlfriend, who always pretended not to recognize Angela even when her name was printed right there in bold letters) to deposit half her pay and give her the rest in ten-dollar bills.

After she picked up her lunch (Friday was shrimp salad on wheat toast with lettuce, tomato, and red onion with a thin slice of cheesecake to celebrate the end of her workweek), it pleased her to sit at her switchboard station and confirm her hair appointment with Mickey, who had a tendency to take walk-in perms or dye-jobs if she didn't check in. Angela's hair was a bit fine, so Mickey kept it short with a slight wave and highlights to give her hair more bounce. Nothing obvious or overdone, of course. Father Peralta wouldn't let her leave the confessional on Saturdays with anything trashy. Mickey had been in business on Court Street over twenty years. Angela chose his place for its name, *A Cut Above*, which was exactly how Mickey made her feel. Angela always thought of her sisters as she left the salon. They didn't have weekly hair appointments, so they had to wash and set their own hair, when they had time.

Angela met the other answering-service girls for dinner and a movie, then walked back to Junior's for two cheesecakes, one deluxe with chocolate chips, for her family. Angela still lived in the apartment she was raised in, with Paulie and Matt, her two unmarried brothers. Her other siblings lived in the same building, each taking an apartment as they married and started families of their own. Their mother had wanted her children and grandchildren close, and the landlord trusted they wouldn't make trouble.

Angela didn't feel like going home just yet. She wanted to hold on to all that James Bond adventure for just a little while longer. Her sisters never asked about the movies she saw, and they laughed at her when she came home overly excited. Angela thought it would do her sisters good to get out occasionally, but they *don't have time for such foolishness*.

Angela enjoyed doing many things they considered foolish, including working outside the neighborhood, even after a union packing job at the pencil factory opened up. She was a longshoreman's daughter and respected the hard physical work that he had done (that all but one of her brothers did now), but she preferred office work. Angela didn't mind the bus ride every morning and evening, and as much as she loved coming back to the neighborhood and her family, downtown Brooklyn was a completely different world. Angela thought it would be good for her family to see more of the world, like she did.

Her sisters thought she was too adventurous, and according

to them, this was the reason she remained unmarried (as if single men only lived in Greenpoint and Williamsburg). They all thought she'd find a husband *if only she spent more time in the neighborhood.* Angela didn't blame her sisters for this. They had worked at the church or along the docks, and met their husbands through work, all except Grace, who got married before she finished her second year of high school (but the family never talked about that anymore). Angela couldn't really say why she hadn't married, but she wouldn't blame it on her work. She spent most of her day answering and taking messages for doctors, salesmen, and small-business owners. If she wanted a husband, there were plenty of available men on the other end of the line to choose from. The answering service lost a girl that way every few months, as regular as the seasons.

Thinking about these things made Angela walk faster, but it was good to use up her excess energy. Fulton Street still had plenty of foot traffic, even if she was the only woman out alone. Her brothers would be upset if they found out (and whenever she did anything the family might consider questionable, she always managed to be seen by someone they knew). She swung her packages as she walked, thinking of the casinos and the diamonds in the movie, and how bright and exciting everything looked in Las Vegas. Angela often saw things in movies that she would like to see herself, but to cross the whole country she would have to fly, and no one in the family had ever been on a plane. Angela had her own passport, so she *could* fly anywhere she wanted. She used it for her cruise to Bermuda with her girlfriends two years ago. Angela had loved every minute of that vacation, even the part when she was seasick and the doctor came straight to her cabin with pills that made her better. At the casino onboard, she won almost two hundred dollars at the blackjack table, even though she was a first-time player. Her family didn't approve of gambling, so she never mentioned that part of the cruise to them. Angela had liked playing blackjack, and she wanted to see all those fancy casinos with their showgirls and famous singers.

Her sisters, Alma especially, would say it was a sin to visit such a godless place. Still, a Las Vegas vacation might be worth their disapproval. When she confessed the blackjack money to Father Peralta, he only made her say two extra Our Fathers as penance.

When she was ready, Angela took a taxi home. Her sisters weren't sitting on the stoop waiting for her as they normally did, even when she came home after midnight, which they all hated because it made them worry. The building was a four-story brick tenement with seven apartments, two on each floor except the first, which had the laundry room instead. It was the perfect size for their family, and her brother Paulie often joked that he, Matt, and Angela had to remain single because moving the entire family to a larger building would be too difficult. Angela and her two brothers lived on the third floor, but the only lights on in front were from Rose Anna's apartment above them, so Angela brought the cakes there. The women were crowded around the table, not a husband or child in sight.

"What's wrong?" Angela cleared papers to make room for the dessert, and her youngest sister Grace, propped against the kitchen doorway (where she could show off the curvy body men admired and women envied), brought out plates, forks, and a knife.

"Box & Paper shut down," Donna said. "My poor Pete and Tommy, Matt, Frankie, and Burt all out of work, no notice, only two weeks severance."

"They'll find something new," Angela said. "Real soon, you'll see." She passed out slices of cake, pleased she had a special offering when everyone needed comfort.

❋

On the bank line two weeks later, Angela changed her routine for the first time in ten years. She handed Mary Francis her passbook. "Your deposit slip?" she asked, all-business, like she'd never sat down for Sunday dinner with Angela and her family.

"I want all of it this week, Mary Francis O'Shea." Angela used her full name to remind her that nobody from the neighborhood would ever call her Fran, no matter what she wrote on the plastic nametag pinned to her fancy ruffled blouse (the same blouse Angela had admired in the A&S last week, but had passed on because the price was too dear). Angela thought lavender was a terrible choice for a redhead. A blouse like that belonged on her sister Donna, who had thick, black hair, which she still kept long. Angela wouldn't even put that color on Grace, who had chestnut coloring and a forgiving figure. It just proved money couldn't buy good judgment.

That night Angela went straight home after the movie. Her brothers were rarely at home on a Friday night, but Matt had taken to brooding in front of the TV in their father's old armchair. Her brother-in-law Pete and his son Tommy were now loaders at the brewery where Paulie worked, but Matt hadn't left the house since he was laid off.

"Have you eaten?" Angela asked. "Rose Anna brought us sauce the other night."

No answer.

"I have leftover chicken cutlets in the fridge, I'll fry them up real quick." He waved her off and raised the volume on the TV.

"Okay, well…I just thought I'd let you know that I left Paulie a check to cover our share this month. Just till you get on your feet." Her brothers had always paid the rent without her, and she expected Matt to fuss about how a man had to earn his own way. It was hard to be sure he even heard her, but Angela couldn't mention it so casually a second time.

❋

The catsup factory off Huron was the next to go, locking out Vince and Carmine without warning one Monday morning. The company blamed the union for erasing their profits. They wrote it that way on the notice they plastered on all the doors, directly above the chains. There had been talk during last winter's strike how the machinery needed to be retooled to manufacture vacuum-sealed packets. *Unfortunately wage increases have made it more cost effective to abandon production.* Eighty-five employees were permanently laid off by mimeographed signs that smelled of freshly pressed ink. Representatives from the union local arrived, but they were too stunned to offer anything beyond a rage of words. They wanted to sue for severance, but first they had to write headquarters for advice. Nobody had ever seen a factory shut down on the sly before, and nobody much liked the example they were setting. The factories along the East River were of an age. They all needed retooling.

Angela skipped the movie that Friday. Rose Anna was fighting mad about her husband Vince being treated so shabby after fifteen years, and her anger unsettled the whole family. Rose Anna and Donna were the closest in age (less than nine months apart after Rose Anna insisted on being born early), but Rose Anna's temperament was as stormy as Donna's was mild. "So close, yet so far apart," their mother had said. Angela wanted to do anything she could to make things better for everyone. She thought about bringing home cheesecake, but it seemed too extravagant under the circumstances. Instead, she caught the bus to the Northside and picked up some Genoa salami, a wedge of provolone, and three loaves of the peasant bread with the good crust and soft middle everyone liked.

The subway stop at Lorimer was roped off, so Angela had to walk the rest of the way home in her work heels. She thought her offering was worth the effort, until Rose Anna greeted her with, "Did you do something new with your hair today, Angela?"

This made everyone look her way and notice that her hair was styled exactly as it always was. Angela quietly tossed off a Hail Mary to the Virgin to keep herself from reminding Rose Anna that she bought Tessa's big-girl bed for her birthday just last month. She wouldn't kick her sister when she was down (not when Rose Anna would probably march right into Tessa's room and make the poor sleeping child give it back). Angela would do right by her niece. She would turn the other cheek, but she'd get her hair set every week till Judgment Day, as long as she kept working and earning money all her own.

"I'm worried about Matt," Angela said, to change the subject. She looked to Donna for support. Donna was the family peacemaker with Mama gone now.

"Hugo said your father used to sulk when things didn't go his way," Nelly, her sister-in-law, said. Nelly never meant to be unkind, so no one, Rose Anna included, corrected her. Silence at the table was so unusual that Angela noticed her other sister-in-law (Mitzi, who simply lacked kindness) stirring her tea, spoon clinking rhythmically against the cup, as she tried to rein in her delight. Angela couldn't understand why her brothers, raised by and around such good women (and while she could find fault with each of her sisters, they were all good women), had chosen so poorly.

"Matt's not sulking," Angela said, after it was clear that no one would defend either him or their father.

"He's grieving," Rose Anna said. "He lost the only job he ever had. We should let him mourn it." Rose Anna looked at Angela. "Don't fuss over him. Just let him shake this off on his own."

Angela disagreed, but there were too many heads nodding around the table. She couldn't argue with them all.

❋

When the wire and cable factory burned down, Angela sensed the bad times they were facing might not take a turn for the better, as they always had before. The fire trucks set a 5:30 alarm, but the men who got dressed and went to help were turned away. Despite the tang of burning metal in her nostrils, Angela left for work believing it was a minor fire. Ash fell in flakes when she returned home.

She reversed direction, walking toward St. Anthony's to light a candle. The soot was thick along the white stone steps, leaving trails of footprints going to and from the side door. The church kept the front doors locked now on weekdays, and even the side entrance would close in an hour. Her mother used to sit in the front pew and pray late at night. She had liked how quiet it was then, how dim and still, with the incense burned out but still lingering in the air. Angela was glad her mother didn't live to see it shut up tight, as if God himself was afraid.

Angela was too late. All the candles were already lit, even the dollar offerings that were supposed to burn for a week straight. She didn't stay to pray. She didn't want hers to be the last in a line of pleas, with no candle burning to bring attention to her prayers. She chided herself for thinking of God's time like a day at the answering service (when it was so much harder to be ever-sweet and helpful late in the day), even as she slipped through the door and walked toward the falling ash, home.

Grace's Burt stumbled out of the corner bar, calling to Angela as she passed the storefront window with its torn, faded-through curtain. She didn't think grown men with mouths to feed had any business paying jacked-up prices to get all liquored up. He smelled of firecrackers dipped in beer.

"Nothing's been the same since the Navy Yard went," Burt said, weaving closer than he'd been when they danced at his wedding. "It ain't the same here no more."

The fire had taken his third job in four years, and Angela had no answer for him, no words that wouldn't sound hollow or false. She gripped his forearm and helped him up the stoop, giving each bell three short, steady rings to signal she needed help with lifting. Normally when her nephews came they carried groceries up the stairs, but it wasn't the first time that Frankie or Jude had helped an uncle or their own father up the stairs and into bed.

The fire was blamed on the men who lived by the abandoned factories along the docks. They slept in refrigerator boxes, used the river as their toilet, and set fires in the rusted metal garbage cans chained to the wooden pier. The wire and cable company took the insurance payment and relocated to an industrial park opening in Delaware. They got more than the equipment and property had been worth, so overnight security at the remaining factories fell victim to budgeting shortfalls. The men who still had work took turns guarding the buildings at night, so another fire wouldn't advance the inevitable.

❂

Angela economized by packing her own lunch and eating at her desk, instead of going out with the rest of the girls. Today, the bread was soggy and the lettuce limp. She caved in to Betty's *Angela, pleeaasse.*

She ordered the grilled cheese special at the diner for $2.99 with fries and a Tab, guilt-free. She deserved a social life, and she hadn't been to the movies in over a month.

"We're all going to Vegas for Lincoln's birthday weekend, and we need a fourth for the room," Betty said.

"I can't spend the money," Angela said.

"It was your idea," Pam said. "You have to come."

"Las Vegas?" Angela asked. "When have I ever mentioned Las Vegas?"

"When we saw *Diamonds Are Forever,*" Jackie said. "You said we should all go together, like Bermuda."

"You didn't even work here when we went on the cruise," Angela snapped. Somehow, being responsible for the trip made her angry she couldn't go. "We saw that movie, what…two years ago?" It seemed like ages, but she still remembered how restless she felt afterwards, like every life ought to be an adventure.

"We have almost five months, we can sign up and pay on time." Betty was both beautiful and persuasive. Angela thought she should be working at the A&S, selling cosmetics or perfume. Angela considered the trip all through her meal. She ate her sandwich in small, thoughtful bites, trying to find a way to justify the expense. Maybe she could do some weekend shifts at the service. It was only for a few days—the overtime alone could pay for it.

"Think of it as a Christmas present for yourself," Betty said.

Angela thought she deserved a special gift, but then she pictured all the shabby trees on Christmas morning. Good times and bad, the family always made birthdays and the holidays special. Vegas would be awful if it meant her nieces and nephews went without. She would work the overtime, make sure they each had something they wanted under the tree. Seeing their faces on Christmas morning would be like a trip back to childhood. She shook her head, banishing all thoughts of Las Vegas. She'd save all that glitter for the tree the boys brought home for her each year.

❄

Two of the breweries shut down next, the second only three weeks after the first. City traffic was to blame. Shipping had shifted away from the river and onto the highways and rail yards. Truckers lost too much time driving into and out of the city, and there were no freight trains with direct access to the harbor. Still, Angela didn't understand. The way things were going, the breweries seemed to have more local business than ever.

Her brother Paulie had been laid off this time, and Angela left work early when she heard. She found him sitting at the table, drinking Jim Beam from the bottle.

"Not you, too," she said, kicking off her shoes as she crossed the threshold. She wanted to rip off her pantyhose but could never do something so common in front of the boys. "I expect you to have more sense in your head."

"I'm celebrating," he said. He wiped his mouth with the back of his hand and capped the bottle. "Sort of."

"I thought you liked the work?" Paulie was a brewmaster; he made sure of the beer's quality and taste. He didn't earn too much more than the others, but it wasn't back-breaking work loading and lifting.

"They didn't let me go."

Paulie twirled the bottle until Angela put it back in the pantry, on the floor behind her cleaning products. She felt too tired to be stooping, but she didn't like having liquor in the house. When her parents were alive, the boys never brought it home. She'd go to the church tomorrow and pay at the rectory for a memorial mass, one each for her mother and father. The family needed all the heavenly help they could muster. "They're shutting down," she said. "What can you do for them?"

"I can move to Missouri."

"What?" Angela filled the water kettle for tea. "Is that out on Long Island? My friend Nancy from the answering service moved there after she got married. The house is surrounded by potato fields. It takes half an hour to get to the grocery store, and she hates driving just like you do."

"It's a state, Sis. Missouri. Like New York and New Jersey."

"What's it near?" She left the kitchen, the kettle still in her hand.

"I don't know. It's in the middle somewheres. I was gonna borrow the encyclopedia from Mitzi and look it up."

"They're old. Her father bought them for her when she was in school." (That didn't stop her sister-in-law from acting high and mighty over them.)

"Missouri hasn't moved in the last twenty years," Paulie said.

"I'm just saying some of the kids got in trouble using them." She banged the kettle onto the burner, then had trouble turning on the gas. Her hands were shaking, and she needed a cigarette. She hadn't smoked in three years. "Things change and everything."

Paulie came up behind her, "Things *are* changing, Ange."

She shrugged away from him, sat at the table, and helped herself to one of his cigarettes. When she couldn't get the match to light, he lit one for her. "Where's Matt? Is he home?"

"He's always home," Paulie said.

Angela inhaled like the smoke was oxygen: "Ask him if he wants tea."

"You can come with me if you want," Paulie said. "I think you should."

Angela ignored the whistling kettle, and took a few more

drags before she stubbed out the cigarette. Her throat was already burning from the smoke. She had forgotten that part. She skirted past Paulie, walked through her bedroom into the living room where Matt watched *Columbo*, the sound barely audible. He didn't seem to be looking in the TV's direction. "Do you want some tea? Paulie and I are both having some."

Angela counted to ten, in English and Italian, the way her mother used to when she lost patience with her children. "Mattie, come sit with us for a while. You don't have to talk if you don't want to. Just sit with us, just you, me, and Paulie. Please."

She blocked the television screen, but this didn't bother him. "Are you watching this?" she asked. When he didn't answer, she shook him, as if he might be asleep. He didn't squirm from the pressure of her hand, although he had never liked to be touched. Angela moved back to the set, switched it off, and snuffed out the last bit of light in the room. Matt didn't give any signal that he knew she was in the room with him, deliberately getting in his way. She waited one minute more, then left him alone in the dark.

When she came back, Paulie had already poured the tea. There were only two cups. It was his certainty that made her bury her face in her hands. They hadn't been raised to cry. God's will was mysterious and absolute. Hardship was meant to be endured. Paulie took hold of her shoulders and guided her into a chair. He pushed the hair from her eyes, and held onto her head like he was trying to give a benediction. "What did you expect? Every night, you go in there like he's just gonna be normal again."

"I expect you to help him," she snapped. "He's your brother."

"He needs more help than we can give him." Paulie's voice was hard, and this surprised her. She expected him to bend. It was what they did for each other.

"Families stay together, especially in hard times." She didn't know what he was thinking. What would he do there? Who would he live with? How could he stand to be alone? She was afraid for him, for the foolishness of his pride. Life was difficult enough with your family all around you.

He slapped the table, and tea sloshed over the rims of both cups. Of course, there were no saucers. "You do too much already."

"You'd rather see your own go without?"

"They're not ours. *We* didn't *make* those babies," he said. "Think of yourself, before they take and they take and leave you with nothing."

"If it comes to that," she said resolutely. "I'll pray it doesn't." Angela sipped her tea. Paulie always put in too little milk and too much sugar, the way *he* liked it. She supposed she ought to be grateful Paulie didn't consider himself above making tea. Her mother had believed in women's work and men's work, and her father, permanently stooped from years on the loading docks, boasted how he never once set foot in his wife's kitchen.

"What are there—three more breweries left?" she asked.

Paulie sighed, eyes focused on his tea. They drank slowly and without conversation. When Angela cleared the cups from the table, he said, "I'll check with the others, if they're hiring."

❀

The oil truck was delivering this week, Alma had a toothache she couldn't cure with her daily novenas, and Frankie and Tommy needed the filing fee for the transit workers' entrance exam. Angela scribbled figures on a blank deposit slip as she waited, trying to come up with a sum she could spare. She had become expert at separating the mandatory from the merely required payment. The last few pages of her passbook recorded only withdrawals, and Angela wanted to reverse the trend, make at least a token deposit.

"Angela," Mary Francis prompted. "It's your turn." She was smiling. It made Angela suspicious. In the years-long war of the bank line, there had never been a truce.

"I'm not ready yet," she said. She stepped aside to let the next customer forward, but Mary Francis waved her over.

"You can fill it out here."

She decided she would deposit $50. It was bold, possibly

selfish, but it made her feel good. Angela handed the slip to Mary Francis, and saw that her nails, usually so carefully manicured—French style, with the white tips—were bitten down and untended.

"No manicure this week?" Angela asked. Mary Francis smiled weakly, and stamped and processed her check. Her blouse was faded, and her skirt had a safety pin at the waist. Angela had always considered Mary Francis too proud. It never occurred to her that she treated Mary Francis the way her sisters sometimes treated her, like she didn't deserve her weekly hair appointment or a night out at the movies.

When Mary Francis handed back her passbook, Angela said, "You're doing it, too, aren't you?"

Mary Francis stiffened. Angela steeled herself for a biting remark about assuming her family's troubles were universal. Mary Francis straightened her blouse, and patted her hair. "Times are tough," Mary Francis said flatly. "What choice do we have?"

Angela felt her own hand going to her hair, but she checked herself. The war between them ended with a helpless nod.

❊

Matt slipped in the bathroom the day Angela celebrated her fifteenth anniversary with the answering service. After work, Angela modeled the leaf-shaped gold earrings she had received for each of her sisters. While she sat with Donna, eating cannoli that Jude had brought home from his part-time job bussing tables at a cafe in the city, it was Paulie who found Matt unconscious on the floor, and it was Alma and Grace who scrubbed his blood from the tiles after the ambulance had taken him away.

Angela spent a week in the hospital chapel, until she knew he would live. Her prayers were only half-answered. Matt refused to cooperate in his recovery. He was given a psychiatric exam and diagnosed with severe depression. Now Angela had a word for what was wrong with Matt, but it didn't bring her comfort. *Depressed* seemed to be the kind of thing a man ought to shrug off. She wanted a word she didn't know, something with so many syllables she would have to learn to pronounce it right. That kind of illness would help her forgive all the pain and worry he had caused. But Matt didn't care about her suffering or her forgiveness. He didn't care about counseling or outpatient therapy. He didn't care about getting better for his family, and he didn't care about ever coming home.

❀

Angela returned to work after Matt was transferred to the state hospital in Queens. She worked double-shifts to make up the time she had lost, and some weekends. She told everyone it was for the money, but she couldn't set foot beyond the front room of her apartment. Every night she came home, unlocked the door, and sat at her table. Someone was always there to bring her tea and talk with her about her day, yet she never left that chair. The bathroom was just through the kitchen, and Matt's bedroom was within arm's reach of the far side of the table.

On the subway ride home, Angela told herself she would do more than just drink tea with Rose Anna or Alma or Grace before excusing herself to go down to Donna's to change and go to sleep. That was what Angela did now, she worked and she slept, in her sister's apartment, on a single princess bed she bought her oldest niece, Rae, on her fourth birthday, with her very first paycheck from the answering service. Angela even skipped her hair appointments. She never went anywhere, so why spend money that could be put to better use?

When she opened the door, an elderly woman she didn't recognize was already sitting in her chair, drinking her tea. Angela wasn't used to seeing strangers in her home. It could only mean more bad news. They were never friendly with outsiders. Even Angela, who had made many friends at the answering service over the years, had never brought them home or let her two worlds mix in any way.

Donna was propped against the kitchen doorway, scowling at

her feet. Mitzi, who sat with the woman, called, "Angela's home."

Donna came to Angela's side, squeezed her hand, and walked out without letting go. Angela was pulled toward the steps. Donna took a deep breath, and dropped Angela's hand as she exhaled. "What's wrong?" Angela asked.

Donna shook her head and tromped down the stairs. Angela had never heard her sister stomp her feet that way. Donna reached her apartment and slammed the door, the echo rising two flights.

When she turned around, Paulie was in the doorway. "I didn't expect you home so soon. Do you want tea?"

Mitzi picked up her tea cup and the stranger's, Matt's '69 Mets cup, which belonged in the pantry until he returned. "My sister-in-law's home early today. Why don't we finish next door? There's a nice breeze through my window at night."

Angela watched them leave, then took her usual seat. Paulie placed a cup in front of her. "No overtime today?"

"Who was that?" Angela asked, coming half out of her chair before sitting back down. "What's wrong?"

"Nothing." Paulie pushed the cup closer. "Relax. Drink your tea."

She pushed the cup away. "What's wrong? Something's happened to Matt..." She stood again, too quickly, and her knees buckled. She clutched the table and knocked over the cup. Tea ran off the tablecloth and sloped toward the door. "Is he—"

"No!" Paulie said. "It's just me. I did something you...might not like."

"What?" She balled the wet tablecloth in her fists. "Who is that woman?"

"She's here to look at the apartment. She's nice. Just her husband and a grandson, maybe Vinny's age."

"*This* apartment?" Angela rasped, her throat constricting.

"I can't take it any more. Not after Matt. I'm going to Missouri."

Her mouth opened, but she couldn't speak. She pointed to her chest, meaning *What about me?*

"There are too many bad memories for you here," he said. His eyes were focused just beyond her. It was the trick he used as a child whenever their father was angry with him. "You'll be better off with Donna and Pete."

"You—," but she still couldn't speak. Angela shook her finger, thinking *shame*. She was ashamed of him. She turned and stumbled out the door. Grace and Alma were sitting on the top step. Alma rubbed her rosary while Grace stretched her collar over her chin. They sandwiched her as she walked down to Donna's. Rose Anna sat at the table, head down as she pulled at the hem of her housedress. Donna stood in the kitchen doorway again, still scowling at her feet. They were either upset beyond speech or no longer believed that words could offer any comfort, but they wouldn't leave her side until she told them it was okay to go.

✸

"Please, Ange, don't leave it like this. Come out and say goodbye," Paulie pleaded through the door. He was leaving for the airport, and she was hiding from him in Pete and Donna's bathroom. Her bathroom now. Tomorrow, an elderly Polish couple and their grandson would move into her apartment, the apartment she was raised in, the apartment her parents had lived and died in, the apartment Paulie and Matt had ripped from her, each in their own way. It was the first time in ten years that someone not related to them would rent in the building they had made their own. Angela had tried to get Donna's daughter Rae and her husband to take it, but Rae said she liked being "Close, but not too close" to the family.

Donna and Pete only had Jude left at home, with their two older children out of the house. She had a bedroom to herself, and Donna did all the housework Angela had been responsible for when she lived with the boys. She had to admit it was nice to come home from work and not have to cook, scrub the toilet, or wash and iron three sets of work clothes.

"You can't refuse to say goodbye," Paulie said.

He was refusing to stay, so she was refusing him right back.

"This is it, Angela." He thumped the door two times. "I'm leaving now."

The front door opened and closed. He was leaving, actually leaving. She didn't understand how this could still surprise her. She opened the door, and the kitchen was empty. "Mother-fucking son-of-a-bitch."

It surprised her still.

"You plan to kiss me with that gutter mouth?" Paulie said. He was sitting in the chair closest to the door. "You're as gullible as the kids."

She had cursed aloud. Father Peralta would give her a half-dozen Hail Marys tomorrow. She wondered how many Paulie would get for his sins. He hadn't been to Mass in years.

"I know this hurts you, and I'm sorry," he said. "I wish you would change your mind and come with me."

She didn't think there were many priests in Missouri—what if he got married and his wife wasn't Catholic?

"Angela, what more can I say?"

She stamped her foot. She didn't want him getting married to any woman she didn't know, Catholic or not. "So go, or you'll miss your plane."

Paulie hooked his arm around her waist and pulled her to him, like one of his women at the bar. "I'm going to miss *you*, you dope."

She hugged back, almost against her will. After a minute she let go, also against her will.

He looked beyond her again, and said, "I'll send money for the others, when I can."

Now both her brothers were lost to her. Paulie would keep his promise at first, but each check would be spaced out just a few weeks longer than the last, until they couldn't be predicted or relied upon. Then they would stop. He would cut them off completely, forget he was the second-born son of Emilio and Luisa; brother to Elio, Donna, Rose Anna, Alma, Hugo, Angela, Matt, and Grace; godfather to Tommy, Vinny, and Enza; and uncle to fifteen girls and five boys.

Angela knew it then, and she was right.

Beer Money

*R*ose Anna wiped her palms against her apron, and the red-striped seersucker stayed bunched in her fists as she paced her kitchen. The hammering from the barges anchored off the river had given her a headache that pounded to the carpenters' rhythm. With the bicentennial this year, Macy's fireworks were supposed to be extra spectacular, and Rose Anna's rooftop, a half-block from the river, offered the best view in the city. The barges faced the rich folks in Manhattan, but they were anchored in Brooklyn and stayed close enough during the display that ash fell around them, dusting the streets as far as Manhattan Avenue. There wasn't a family in the neighborhood that didn't deserve this yearly front-row seat. Rose Anna only prayed that when the fireworks came, they all had something left to celebrate.

She lapped around the living room, the only thing in motion against the dead summer heat. She switched the television on and then off again—she wouldn't get caught up in soap-opera problems, not when she had so many of her own—then returned to the kitchen so she could check the sauce simmering on the stove. Behind the pot was the same faded, stained paper she'd been scrubbing for fifteen years and could never rub clean. If the rumors were true and the brewery shut down, she'd be scrubbing that same paper and the nicked, bleached-out floor until she was just as worn-through.

Rose Anna lifted the lid, and the trapped air rose soft and

warm over her face. It was the gentlest touch of her day. That was the reason she always volunteered to make the sauce, giving her sisters some freedom from their stoves. She stirred, then checked the oven temperature. Her thermometer read 200 degrees, 150 degrees lower than its setting when summer already gave the oven a head start. She kicked the door closed, stirred her sauce once more before replacing the lid, and sat down to drink her cup of tea and smoke. She believed hot drinks and hot steam cooled you down eventually.

She took a long drag of her cigarette and exhaled a few of her jangled nerves. She had a reputation for being demanding—and maybe she was, compared to the rest of her family—but she didn't want much. A house. Nothing fancy. Two or three bedrooms, with a little yard so she could plant a garden, grow her own vegetables and herbs. Maybe plant some pretty flowers in window boxes, rest a small table underneath a shady tree. But she'd trade that tree for appliances that worked the way they were supposed to, without coaxing or special tricks or rest breaks between use. Rose Anna was as old as her stove, and she didn't have the luxury of breaking down. Just thinking about it made her suck through her cigarette faster, when she wanted to savor it, make it last. She and her Vince had agreed only one carton each every month, so they could try to make that down payment, even in hard times. They had a special home buyer's savings account down at the bank, and they tried to put away a little something with each paycheck. With the kids growing like magic beans and something always needing fixing or replacing, their balance hadn't come to much yet. The thought of what might be coming made her light another cigarette from the butt of the first.

She checked her sauce again, then went to check on her kids from the windows at the front of the apartment. She had six rooms and four windows, two each at the front and rear. Perpetual twilight, just dark enough to hide the chipped paint and cracked walls, tears in the furniture and tape on the floor. Vince had promised her a house, but the brewery was the last place to work along the docks.

If it closed, she might die in this shithole. And be grateful for it. It was hard to imagine something worse, but their luck seemed to be shifting in that direction. Vince was a good husband, responsible and hard working, but he was a broad-shouldered longshoreman with a sixth-grade education. The whole city was running short on opportunities for that kind of man.

Her sister Donna was supposed to be minding the kids. She was clustered across the street with the other women, watching the brewery while the children played stickball in the street. The brewery trucks were coming and going, and the kids were dodging them instead of breaking up the game.

Rose Anna banged on the window with her fist, but she was four floors up. The thought of a round-trip on the stairs in this heat made her want to lie down and nap, but her niece Lina slipped on an oil slick right in front of an oncoming truck. Rose Anna's oldest, Vinny, pulled her away from the wheels. A dozen mothers had their heads turned in the opposite direction, worried about feeding kids who might be killed if she didn't get down there to hustle them off the street.

Rose Anna scattered the kids like chickens, clucking at them while she stomped through the street. They ran from her outstretched arms and re-formed in clusters just beyond her reach. She called to her sister, but Donna was still gossiping with the other women.

Rose Anna muttered curses at them all, but she stopped when she saw the entrance to Schaeffer. There were men carting off kegs in their cars, in wheelbarrows, on go-carts and little red wagons.

"Rheingold dumped the extra beer in the river when they shut down. At least Schaeffer's giving it away," Donna said.

"Lord help us, they're the last. Least they can do is get them all drunk and stupid on the leftovers," said Margie, the widow who lived in 33.

That didn't sound right to Rose Anna, but she didn't want to speak out against the group. At least, not without a reason. Her niece, the only one from her husband's side, rode past on her bike and stopped by her cousin Tessa, Rose Anna's youngest. Tessa and Franca called Lina over, but she waved and kept playing stickball with the boys. Lina and Franca were best friends, as their mothers had been as children. Her nieces proved it was still good to live here, close to both families, in a neighborhood with second-generation friendships.

Franca's bike stayed glued to her hip while she talked. Rose Anna never saw her without it, and the purple paint, streamers, and pretty white basket with matching purple flowers had given both Tessa and Lina terrible bicycle envy. Not that Tessa had ever asked for a bicycle. Rose Anna wondered how many cigarettes it would take to buy something that fine, to see her own child's face riding by looking so red-cheeked and happy. Sometimes Rose Anna wanted better for her children so bad she wished she'd never had them.

Her apron was balled in her fists again. She sighed, shook out her fingers, and walked over to the girls. Tessa greeted her with, "We're not doing nothing, Ma."

"How's Nana doing, Franca? I haven't seen her on the stoop in a few days."

"Her gout's bad again, so she can't make it down the stairs."

"Tell her I'll get up to visit just as soon as I can. Could you ask your father to have a look at my stove when he gets a chance? The temperature's off."

"Yes, Zia," Franca said.

Rose Anna patted her niece on the cheek and turned away. "Tessa, if you're not doing nothing, feel free to run upstairs and clean your room," she called out behind her.

She walked back to the women, who hadn't stirred. She watched the alley with them for a few minutes. A few men trickled out without any beer. Rose Anna tried to understand why some men carted off a dozen kegs and some men none. Seniority? Old Bill Hawkins was walking out empty-handed, and he'd worked at the brewery so long he said he hated the sight and smell of beer. That didn't sit right with any severance she could think of. If he didn't want to drink it, he could sell it later, right?

"They're not giving it away for free." Rose Anna kicked the curb, the nearest target. "They're letting 'em buy it for cheap with their salaries."

Donna, who knew when to ignore her sister, had also learned to trust her over the years. Rose Anna was harder to please than the rest of them, and she was always the most right about things going wrong. "Did you pay the rent yet?"

Rose Anna said, "Come on, I need to think." Donna followed her across the street and sat down beside her on the stoop.

"You don't think they'd spend it all, do you?" Donna asked. Rose Anna's legs were shaking, making her hair bounce and shimmer in the light. "I mean, not their last, they wouldn't…"

"Yeah, like they've never drank it all away before," Rose Anna said, in that voice that made her sisters feel stupid in a way even their husbands couldn't manage.

Rose Anna grabbed Donna by the shoulders. "We need to get in there and get the money away from Fat Louie before their shifts end."

"He won't give us the money," Donna said. She tried to use the stupid voice, but it didn't work right.

"Not us." Rose Anna bit roughly at her thumb nail. "Vinny, Lina, get over here now." She pointed at Lina, the youngest child in the family. "Her."

Donna said, "But, she's a *beast*."

"She's got something. It'll work on Fat Louie."

"What, Ma?" Vinny kept Lina slightly behind him, shielding her. Rose Anna was proud that her boy was prepared to take the brunt of whatever he thought was coming. He was a good boy, and she thought he'd do right when he was grown.

"You know what Fat Louie looks like?"

"Yeah."

"I want you to go in and ask for your father's and your uncles' last pay. Tell him I sent you, and if he doesn't give it to you, I'll remember. Show respect, but tell Fat Louie I'll remember till I'm dancing on his grave."

"Ma…" Vinny stuffed his hands in his jeans and rocked on his heels, afraid she'd dance on his grave, too, if he disrespected her.

"You're taking Lina with you. She's your secret weapon. You tell him what I said, and you leave the rest to her."

"We should ask Grace about this," Donna said. Rose Anna growled at her. Donna had never known humans could make that sound. But then, Rose Anna wasn't acting very human right now. Her own boy looked terrified, although little Lina, who Grace sometimes called Rose Anna Junior, seemed incapable of expressing fear. Even so, Donna tried again. "Rose Anna—"

"*Basta*," Rose Anna said, dismissing her elder sister. She reached out for Lina and pulled her closer. "Listen, honey, I need you to stare, the way you do sometimes when we yell at you. I don't want you to say anything with that smart mouth you've got. You can't do that, *carina*, promise me, right? Just stare and don't blink like you do at Fat Louie and don't stop, even if your daddy or Uncle Vince or Uncle Hugo or Uncle Pete see you and try to make you go home."

Rose Anna pulled out Lina's barrettes and smoothed out her hair. She tucked her shirt in her shorts, and wiped the smudges from Lina's face with her apron. "Your dad or your uncles they might yell at you, but you just have to get stubborn like you do and keep staring. Nobody likes it when you stare that way. When you see Fat Louie—Vinny's going to point him out if you don't know him—you don't worry 'bout no one but him. You just stare, and if you do that, you'll start to make up for all the trouble you cause. You understand me?"

Lina nodded, too dazed by all the words her aunt threw at her to speak or blink. But she was doing exactly what Rose Anna wanted.

Rose Anna turned on Vinny, cleaning him up roughly with some spit and her apron. "You stay clear of your father and your uncles, and if you can't and you see them, you tell them I'll lock 'em all out if they cross me. Every last one of them." She slapped her fists on her thighs for emphasis. "You understand me?"

"Yes, ma'am."

"Go!" Rose Anna commanded.

Lina thought all her problems stemmed from not being born a boy. She spent a lot of time thinking about why she was always in trouble. She didn't think she was bad; she just wasn't very good at girl stuff. She got angry fast, she talked back sometimes, and she had real problems staying clean. She thought the last part made them maddest of all, but it was the hardest one to change. Dirt was everywhere, waiting. She tried real hard not to talk back sometimes, concentrated on it until her head hurt, but they didn't like that either. They said she was staring, but she was just thinking hard, trying not to talk back. She wasn't looking at them at all. It was like she was all inside her head making sure she didn't say nothing but *Yes, ma'am* and *No, ma'am*. When she was in trouble that was all they ever wanted to hear.

She followed Vinny across the street and onto the docks, past the boarded-up envelope factory and in through the side entrance of Schaeffer's loading zone. Vinny made Lina duck behind some crates, wood that smelled like the blind alley where the bad men slept in cardboard at night. She wanted to leave, run away from the smell that made her sick, but she stuck with Vinny like she was told. Aunt Rose Anna stayed mad the longest, and she always let Mama know just how angry she was. Mama didn't like that much. Nobody liked it when Aunt Rose Anna was mad. Besides, if she got sick in front of Vinny, he'd tell all the other cousins that she was still a baby.

Lina watched Uncle Pete pass by on a little truck with long metal hands. Vinny pulled her along the row of crates until they turned the corner and snuck up behind Fat Louie, who wasn't fat but tall. His wallet was fat, because he was The Bookie. Lina didn't know what that meant yet, but she would. She had to be real careful who she asked or else she'd be called a baby. Then she'd get mad and just end up in trouble again.

Lina *hated* being the youngest.

Vinny said, "That's Fat Louie. He gives out quarters sometimes."

Lina nodded, impressed with this information. She was always the last to know something.

"What do you want, kid?"

"My ma sent me. She wants you to give me all the paychecks for the family." Vinny wouldn't look up at Fat Louie. Lina knew that was a mistake. You weren't supposed to look afraid with grown-ups. Being in trouble all the time taught her that much.

"Why didn't she come herself?" he asked.

"I don't know. She's cooking or something."

"Get outta here, before your dad comes and knocks you on your ass."

"She'll be real mad…"

"Broads are always mad about something, kid." Fat Louie patted Vinny on the rear. "Time you learned that."

Vinny stepped back as Lina stepped forward. She looked at Fat Louie, then looked inside her head even though she wasn't mad at anybody.

"Who are you?" Fat Louie asked.

Lina stared, mouth shut like she was told. As Fat Louie moved, Lina moved along with him, three steps to his one.

"She's my cousin," Vinny said.

"The whole freakin' neighborhood's your cousin. Whose girl is she?"

"She's my Aunt Grace and my Uncle Burt's kid. She's only seven."

"What's she doing?"

"I don't know, my ma told her to stare at you."

"What for?" Fat Louie stepped back but Lina inched forward. He was taller than anyone in her family, and he didn't lean down to make it easier. "Is she doing that freaky evil-eye shit?"

"If you give me them, I'll stop saying what my aunt told me to," Lina said. She liked the idea of being an evil-eye girl.

"My ma told her not to say anything," Vinny said.

"She told me to say it on the inside so you wouldn't find out."

Fat Louie tried to hide his body behind a too-small crate. "Your mother's a fucked-up bitch, sending a kid around to jinx me like this."

"She told me it would be doubly bad if you cursed." Fat Louie tripped on a box edge. Lina enjoyed making up lies to tell him. This was like ghost stories under the covers till you were too scared to sleep in your own bed.

"You wait here," he said to Vinny. "You keep the little *strega* with you."

Fat Louie came back and tossed some envelopes at them. Vinny stuck them all deep into the front pocket of his shorts. He took her hand and walked with his other tightly clenched around the money.

Lina wrenched her hand free and skipped ahead of him down West Street. He might have the money now, but she knew that she got it from Fat Louie when Vinny, an older *boy,* was ready to give up and go home for a quarter. She sang, "I did it," over and over to the rhythm of her skipping until she saw Aunt Donna and Aunt Rose Anna circling each other, pacing the length of the stoop, their hands all wild and crazy like when Uncle Matt got sick and went away. She thought *I did it* one last time, until the pleasure she felt drained from her. Something was wrong, and they didn't go themselves. They sent *her.*

Vinny caught up and then passed her, handing the checks over to his mother. She tucked them all inside her housedress. Vinny said, "You told her not to say anything and she told Fat Louie she was giving him the evil eye."

Aunt Donna laughed. Aunt Rose Anna said, "Brilliant," and showered her with kisses. Aunt Rose Anna's cheeks were wet and sweaty.

Aunt Rose Anna never cried. She was the mean aunt, the one who was never afraid. What was so scary about a tall man who got frightened by a little girl? What would have happened if Fat Louie wasn't afraid of her being an evil-eye girl? Did they send her *because* she was so much trouble? She wished she could ask Vinny or even Tessa, but they wouldn't tell her. They liked it too much when she didn't know stuff.

"This goes a long way with me, *carina*, a very long way," Aunt

Rose Anna said, before putting Lina down and wiping both their cheeks with her apron.

Lina wanted to know why Aunt Rose Anna was happy and crying, why this once she wasn't in trouble, and if Fat Louie being The Bookie had something to do with punishing bad little girls.

"The kids aren't going to feed themselves," Aunt Donna said. She pinched Lina's cheek before she went inside.

Rose Anna stood, tugging at Lina's sleeve. "Coming?"

Lina shrugged her off. She didn't like how she felt, how things were so mixed up inside. It was a new kind of dirty.

Rose Anna sat down again. It was getting dark, and the brewery's strobe lights rumbled on. "When I was your age, every building along the docks had lights like those. Watching them light up was like having our own sunrise at sunset."

"I want to see that." Lina looked expectantly down the street, as if their combined will could make it happen.

"I wish you could." Rose Anna watched her niece's mood change, how she brightened at the prospect of a new experience. She would try to yell at Lina less, and she would get Grace to stop telling her she was *too smart for her own good* all the time. There was no such thing, and it was time they all learned that.

Rose Anna's headache returned, although the hammering had stopped for the night. Lina stared at the docks. "You'll get to see the fireworks in a few days." Rose Anna brushed the hair from Lina's eyes, hair that was always tangled despite Grace's constant effort. "You like watching them, right?"

Lina sprang off the stoop, startling Rose Anna with such quick motion. "Teacher taught us a song for the bicentennial. Want to hear?"

Rose Anna swallowed a sigh, and reflexively felt for the checks tucked inside her bra. "Sure, *carina*, sing me your song."

Local *Man*

*F*rom bed, Burt listened to his oldest complain about the water pressure in the shower, how it wasn't ever strong enough to rinse the conditioner from her hair. Unlike her bald father, Nikki had dark, coarse hair that she moved purposefully and well, aware how it bounced and framed her face. Burt hoped she married soon, after a quick courtship, before her groom recognized the shrill regularity of her voice.

His youngest swept through the railcar rooms trying to find whatever item she had lost today. Lina was always in motion. Any knickknacks his wife had accumulated during better times were long gone, victim to Lina's chaos, like the math book and umbrella he replaced last month. Burt never looked at Lina without feeling disappointed, if only because she so clearly made a better boy than his middle child, Anton, who rivaled only Nikki in fussing with his hair, and used his hips in that same knowing way she had. Burt didn't hear him at all, which meant another night when he didn't come home or call. Anton was only fifteen, and Burt was afraid to know the details of his life.

It wasn't their noise but the cold that finally pushed Burt from bed, now that morning wasn't different from any other part of his day. Married twenty years, he had grown used to Grace radiating heat as she slept, a power she'd shut off if she could because it gave him pleasure. Grace had clattered her way through cooking breakfast, and Burt had to dress quickly, before the last clank of the dishes in the sink. His wife wouldn't feed him unless the kids were home to see.

Burt sat next to Lina at the table, but she was finger-counting through her long division. "Why is she doing this now, so late?" he demanded.

"Because your son promised to help her and then never came home," Grace said, in a tone which announced that yet another Borowski man had disappointed this family.

"Why can't you help her, or Nikki?"

"Because your filthy clothes don't wash themselves." Grace's hand stabbed the air obscenely, and Burt waved her off, pointing at their daughter's downturned eyes.

"Beh!" his wife replied.

"Lina!" her cousin Enza shouted from the hallway. "I got a test this morning!"

Lina stood, stuffing her homework into her schoolbag. She glanced at Burt, at his plate, not moving until Grace dropped the egg pan at his elbow. "Tonight I'll help you with your homework," Burt called out behind her.

"Tonight you'll stumble home hours after she's gone to sleep." Grace grabbed the pan and dropped it in the sink. She let the water run before she clomped out the apartment door and upstairs to visit one or all of her sisters in her robe and slippers.

Burt used the lid to strain the pan and scooped watery eggs onto his plate. He wouldn't let her accuse him of wasting food in hard times. Not him, he'd eat every morsel, even though it was wrong for a wife to punish a hard-working man for getting laid-off again. Grace treated him like he was some lazy bum who didn't want to work, but he was a dislocated worker. That was the fancy word for *facocked-by-management* they used down at the Unemployment. Every factory in the neighborhood had upped and left because they feared working men who knew their rights and got themselves organized. Just because his brother-in-law Vince was crazy enough to spend two hours on the subway each way for a non-union loading job at the airport that paid half his usual salary didn't mean Burt was a bad husband if he didn't do the same.

Burt spent fifteen years as a shop steward, and he would face his maker as a union man. No scab work for him. Unite and fight; it was the only way for every working man to protect his right to a decent wage. Not that Grace ever listened. "*Sindacato! Sindacato!*" she said, then covered her ears and blabbed Italian, like they all did when they were angry.

His friends had warned him not to marry a wop, American-born or not. "The bloom grows brighter and fades sooner," they said, and just maybe he should have listened. Not that his Grace wasn't still a knockout. Even after all three kids she had a body that made him go weak from the looking, but she was growing more like her sisters with each passing day. If he was married to any one of them, spending all that time on the subway wouldn't be so bad. He reminded himself of that every time he got to thinking how Vince was working a non-union job, him once being an officer with the Local.

Burt's first mistake as a married man had been agreeing to live in the same apartment building with the rest of them. Five sisters shouldn't live together under one roof, because they had no respect for the locks on the doors that separated them. Truth was they were all lookers, but together they traipsed around as they pleased. No privacy, no respect for a man down on his luck. All they talked about was family, but by family they meant *blood* kin.

A man shouldn't be an outsider in his own home. He shouldn't have to face down his in-laws' disapproval at his own table, sometimes before he had a proper shower and a shave. Burt had been raised respectable, so he knew that was wrong. He had to try and live peaceful with a wife who gabbed his private business to women he had to look back at every friggin' day, never a moment without them or a chance to be just a nuclear family. Everything was about Grace's family, but he had family, too. His parents had passed on, but he had a brother with sense enough to move before the jobs disappeared and the neighborhood went to Hell. He should have moved to Delaware with his brother, forced Grace even when she cried and begged him to please *piacere* please change his mind. Burt was such a good husband he wouldn't make her leave, but Burt's brother was still working steady. Did Grace ever blame herself for what happened? Not when she had all those busybody voices in her ears, telling her everything was his fault.

Her people had always disapproved of him, because he was Polish and older by fifteen years. Maybe a thirty-year-old man shouldn't court a schoolgirl, but he did right by her. Since the wedding, they had barely spoken a civil word to him. If that was family, *beh* to them all.

"Bombed already, Pop?" Nikki asked, as she sat beside him.

"What?" He threw his fork at the plate, splashing bits of egg. "What's this garbage you ask your father?"

"My father only mumbles to himself after he's spent all day and night at the bar," she said, as if they were discussing the weather. "Did you start drinking extra early today, or did you get lucky and wake up still drunk from last night?"

Nikki bent over to tie her laces, and Burt swept her work heels off the table. "Get the street off the table and out of your mouth."

Nikki caught her skidding pump and sent it whizzing past his ear. "Giving Ma crap over Lina's homework. I see you trying to get yourself home at night, with all my friends watching, too."

"Dirty girl!" After twenty years, Burt could talk with his hands, too. He ran them wildly across his throat. "Go off and marry one of them, so he can start forgetting right beside me."

"I won't marry anyone like you," she said.

"Whoever you marry will become me!"

Nikki picked up her other heel and said, "Try not to drink all the rent money away. I work hard for what you steal from my mother."

Burt waved and flipped off the door for several minutes after she left, until his anger reached a more normal level. He left the pan and his plate on the table so Grace would know he ate the meal she had ruined. He found his coat and waited at the door until his sister-in-law had finished scrubbing down the stairs before he hurried out without being seen.

Burt turned automatically toward West Street. He knew every inch of those docks, had sweated, joked, and gambled in every blind nook and corner for thirty-five years, but he wouldn't cross over now. Only the bums, dopes, and whores did business now that the squat, empty factories shielded them from easy view. Even the river smelled worse than it used to, when the smokestacks still pumped soot into the air. Burt sniffed again, puzzled. He never expected humans to outstink machines.

Burt moved over to Huron Street, but he passed the bar and kept on walking. His tab was getting high, and soon Jimmy would get to insisting over it. Burt never once stole money from his wife. Grace always gave it to him whenever Jimmy paid a call to the house. Maybe it was a little like stealing when he took the money and drank at the Polish club down on McGuinness Boulevard, but then Grace didn't have to pay out when Jimmy came around. If Jimmy himself was such a hard ass, he'd take the money straight from Grace, but he always refused. It was "Just a warning."

Jimmy knew he was taking food from the mouths of women and children, Burt *knew* he knew that. If Jimmy was so big and noble, he'd refuse to sell to just about every man in the neighborhood. But did he? No. He kept pouring drinks on credit for them all. Burt just hated a hypocrite. There was no real honor in that kind of man.

Burt was coming upon the park. There were no children playing. That's what those management bastards did to the neighborhood. All those phony politicians with their reporters and cameras following as they promised to keep Brooklyn working, those jackals let them get away with it. Not even the union saw it coming. Burt didn't believe it was greed or backstabbing, though. Not with the union. They knew the river would always be there, and they thought that meant the work would stay, too. Burt had believed the same thing, and he had never been more wrong. Now the kids had nowhere to go because only the punks he saw in their spikes and leather, with their brass knuckles and razor blades, got to play there now. Half the neighborhood was punks, dopes, bums and whores when this used to be a decent place to live and raise your children. Never fancy, but decent. The neighborhood had turned to shit because of men who didn't know what it felt like to break a sweat, or to stand out on the picket line dead winter, fingers frozen to the splinters in your sign so you couldn't drop it even if you wanted to, because that's what you had to do to keep your family warm year after year.

Just thinking about it brought on the thirst real bad.

Burt felt for his wallet and looked inside. He had enough for a drink at the Polish club. A double would settle his nerves and warm him up for the long walk to the Unemployment. They gave him the bus fare coming and going whenever he showed up, and the subway clerks would refund tokens one at a time. Burt would make back the money, get his pittance from the government that helped screw him over.

Grace and her lot acted like he didn't want a new job, but they were dead wrong. Burt wanted one bad, because not working left too much time for thinking. All this thinking just messed him up. Now the thirst was on him hard. He needed a taste to get his head right, and that just wasn't his fault. Watery eggs couldn't sustain any man looking to earn a decent wage for his family.

Burt liked the Polish club, just down the steps from the plumbing-supply store. Burt saw the bill the landlord got for the hair clog in the bathtub last year, and he was sure those plumbers had a good union behind them. The club was unmarked and members-only, but they didn't keep a man at the door. All you really had to be was Polish-looking to get served. Burt liked listening to the language, even though he had forgotten all but a few words. It reminded him of dinners at his grandparents' apartment on Olive Street, of time spent with his own blood kin before they died off or moved away. His younger brother Greg had a house, and in the pictures he sent each Christmas, his Delaware wife and kids looked very respectful.

"I want to toast my brother's family," Burt said to the barman. He had downed his drink too quickly to cure the thirst. "Would you spot a man with good intentions?"

"Cash only," the barman replied without looking up from a pour.

"I'm good for it." Burt pulled his union card from his wallet. "You can hold this until I pay you back."

The barman read the card and tossed it onto the bar. "This and five cents is worth less than a nickel."

Burt placed it carefully back into his wallet so it wouldn't get creased. "You might be too young to know it, but the union did good here for a whole lot a years."

"Of course." The barman swept his arm across the span of the club, half-full at midmorning. "Business is booming." He filled a shot glass to the rim and coated the bottom of Burt's empty with gin when Burt was a bourbon man.

"To the union!" the barman said with a snort.

Burt drank the drops of gin and said, "Unite and fight!" with his empty glass held high. He hoped someone else would raise a glass, but the other men were silent. Mostly they nursed drinks without company or conversation. The chatty old-timers who usually played backgammon weren't here. Burt decided Jimmy's at its worst was still more companionable. Jimmy, for all his puffed-up faults, never made a loyal union man feel stupid.

The Unemployment was 3.2 miles from home, which put him just over the carfare minimum. Burt didn't mind the walk. He was used to working outdoors, good weather or bad. He minded getting sassed by some pup with no respect for the one organization that valued physical labor. But it wasn't just him. To work with your hands, use the God-given strength of your body, had become un-American somewhere between Burt's youth and middle age.

Burt began on the docks right next to his own father as a loader at thirteen, stopping only when he was shipped off to Okinawa during the war. It was farm boys and laborers that beat the Japs and Hitler, back when hard work was expected from a man. *Re-*

spected. What he and all the other working men had done to lose that respect so quickly and completely, Burt couldn't figure out. No matter how much time he had for thinking. The war got won on hard labor, and then the whole country decided it was too big and proud to get its hands dirty.

Burt went to the Polish club to get his head screwed right. It seemed like every plan he made went wrong somehow, but he kept trying. He wasn't ashamed to be a working man. The union taught him that much. It wasn't every man who would walk all this way, just looking to support his family, as ungrateful as they were. Grace never once thanked him for all those years he went off to work each morning. Never one word of appreciation for all those paychecks he handed over, leaving himself barely enough for his own personal expenses. A man needed to get the work off his shoulders before he went home to his family at night. Nothing shameful about getting presentable before walking through the front door. It wasn't supposed to be about who got home for dinner first. It mattered how you acted once you got there. Burt never got any credit for coming home in a good mood. That was just another in a long line of damn shames in his life.

The Unemployment wasn't even crowded anymore. Now that the two extensions had run out, the check lines had shifted to the Welfare. The women handled that, along with the WIC coupons and food stamps. Burt waited ten minutes on a wooden, gray-painted bench before he was allowed to view the job book. Ginty, the young red-headed Irish—always it was someone young and new—handed him a stub pencil and three index cards before he brought out the weighty black ledger that offered so few opportunities. As usual, the only loading jobs were at the airport.

"Nothing union?" he asked.

"Have you taken any of the civil service exams?" The Irish asked. "Those are generally—"

"No high school," Burt said.

"I can refer you for an equivalency class, to prepare you for taking the GED exam."

Burt scratched his head. The Unemployment always made him itchy. He shifted in his seat, wishing his wife could have a go at these chairs with one of her cleaning rags.

Ginty leaned far over his desk. "There are working men like you in my family, with city jobs, some union."

"Isn't there a hiring freeze, with the city going bankrupt and all?"

Ginty nodded, pleased Burt could read a newspaper or understand the nightly news. These college boys confused no high school with kicked-in-the-head stupid. "For the moment, but the exams are still being scheduled," he said. "You can look for a copy of *The Chief* in the periodicals room, down the hall and to your right."

Burt waved him off. "No jobs, and they charge fees for those tests. It's a racket. No self-respecting union would let the city get away with that."

"Well, Mr. Brodsky—"

"Borowski." This boy's poor father broke his back at some city job, probably in the sewers with the other Irish, to get him educated and yet he still couldn't read a file right.

"Yes. Well…" Ginty paused. "You wanted union work and I offered you a suggestion. The city may be going through a rough patch, but don't you want to be on the list when things turn around?"

"I'm fifty-two years old. I could be dead by then."

"Mr. Borowski…"

"I still got no high school." Burt's shrug was conciliatory.

"If you sign up for training and attend regularly, the city will pay a stipend that covers lunch and carfare every day."

"Okay, okay," Burt said, and got up from his chair.

"I can arrange to get you signed up right now," Ginty said, rising with him.

"No, no. First I have to talk with my wife," Burt said, and Ginty nodded. These boys were all big on communication, but they would learn soon enough. Burt had never heard a married man complain about how he and the wife never talked enough.

Ginty nodded, and Burt handed him his voucher to sign. Burt waved off Ginty's handshake and went to claim his tokens.

The cramps were in his legs by the time he reached Jimmy's. Burt took a seat at one of the two tables wedged into the narrow bar, because his legs would go numb if they dangled from the barstool after such a long walk. He risked his health to save the money from two tokens. Grace never appreciated the small things like that.

"Too good for us today, Borowski?" Jimmy asked. Regulars always sat at the bar.

"I can't stay." Burt tried to stamp the pins and needles from his legs. "Just a quick beer."

"I thought you were boycotting beer after Schaeffer went back on its word and shut down the brewery," Mackie said. He worked down at the sugar before they shut most of it down. Burt had thought it was silly to work across town, but Mackie had his job about a year longer than the rest of them. His extensions hadn't even run out yet. Grace had been a whole lot nicer when his unemployment check was still coming.

"So, don't give me Schaeffer," Burt said. "I just need something to pick me up before I head home."

"Haven't carried it since the first time they shut down," Jimmy said. "I don't carry stock from any company that turned its back on Brooklyn."

"You're a good man, Jimmy," Burt said. "You got respect."

Jimmy pointed at the black-and-white in the corner above the bar. "I don't play no Dodgers here, not even when they play the Mets. I remember what it felt like to have them leave that way, all sudden."

"That's when it all started, with the Dodgers," Mackie said. Nods dominoed along the bar.

"The Navy Yard went right after," Burt said, nodding with the others. He stood at the bar, taking a long drink of the beer Jimmy placed in front of the empty stool beside Mackie. "Beginning of the end, and we didn't see it coming."

More nods. Mackie said, "You sweating? Unload."

Burt left his empty on the counter and stepped away from the bar. "No. Got to help the kid. Math."

"The little hellcat?" Mackie asked, and the whole bar laughed. There was a story about his Lina scamming Fat Louie that everyone in the neighborhood had heard, but he blamed his sister-in-law for that nonsense.

"I thought your boy was smart with that stuff," Jimmy said.

"He is," Burt said. "My oldest, too. She got a job typing in the city. Fancy lawyer's office, right out of high school."

"She's a looker," Johnny B. said. He was the youngest of the regulars. Lived with his grandmother. "But she's always got her nose in the air."

"Ever think it's the way you smell?" Jimmy roared at his own joke, slapping his hand against the bar.

"Aaaiyhh," Burt grabbed his thigh. Mackie reached out to steady him. "Charley horse," Burt said.

"You walk to the Unemployment again today?" Jimmy poured a double bourbon and gestured at the stool. "Sit down. This one's on me."

Burt sat, and Jimmy slid the drink his way. He didn't think Anton had ever stayed out two nights in a row, and he was usually real good about Lina. Burt took a small sip, to make the gift last. Jimmy didn't offer too many freebies, so it was best to take advantage. Anton had to come home to change clothes, and if he didn't, well, Burt sometimes forgot how smart Nikki was, too. It wasn't fair to think she couldn't help just because she was a girl. Truth was, Nikki could help Lina with the math better than Burt himself could, so many years out of school and all. Of course, his kids got their math smarts from his side of the family, he was sure of that. Lina would be fine. She probably didn't need much help anyway. Everyone said she was *special* smart. The trouble was in getting her to sit still long enough to get things done. And Grace, for all her faults, kept real close watch on their baby girl.

Burt wasn't sure why he made such a fuss in the first place. Lina would be perfectly fine. To make absolutely sure, he'd leave in an hour. It did a man good to chat with his friends after such a long day. It made him a better husband and father.

Burt reached into his wallet and pulled out a discolored piece of paper with many folds. "Hey Mack, you know I still have a copy of that beer boycott flyer we made down at the Local. Did I ever tell you how I helped with the writing?"

Mama Loves You

*I*n three weeks Tessa would be thirteen, a *teen*ager, and she had the boobs to prove it. Tessa pinched her hand-me-down *Charlie's Angels* sweatshirt, holding the fabric behind her so she could catch her profile in the mirror. Mama had taken away most of her favorite tops, all her t-shirts, even though it was almost May. Tessa wasn't stupid. She knew Mama didn't like seeing how grown-up she was. She stretched the fabric as tight as she could get it, cracking the Kate Jackson decal. Tessa pinned the folds behind her with a clothespin she stole off the line in the basement. Mama might think she was a little girl, but she had a real bra with adjustable straps and two hooks in back, not the elastic training kind that she saw on the other schoolgirls, who could still wear their kiddie undershirts even though most of them were already teenagers. Tessa's bra had both a number and a letter: 32B. Mama made the saleslady measure twice, said, "She just can't be that full already."

"Too full," Aunt Grace whispered to Aunt Angela in the hall last night. "Rose Anna can't see that her baby needs a cup size larger than her own."

Tessa knew Aunt Grace was right, because she could see where the elastic made a line that almost gave her four boobs. Tessa read *Teen* magazine whenever she walked her cousin Enza to the library, so she knew that wasn't right.

Aunt Angela only sighed an answer on the stairway, after coming home from work later than usual. She gave Mama money for an early birthday gift because A&S was having a two-for-one foundations sale. Mama let Tessa stay home from school so they would miss the crowds, and Aunt Grace came along because her bras needed to be special ordered. That made her an expert at getting the right kind. Aunt Grace told Mama that Tessa would end up big like she was, and Mama didn't like hearing that at all. Tessa hoped it was true. Men always looked at Aunt Grace walking, even though she was old.

Tessa liked how the boys noticed her now. It made her stand out, when she never had before. Especially around her cousins. Enza was real smart and nobody could be mean about it because of Jude, Lina was the family baby, and every woman in the neighborhood mothered Franca because hers had died when she was little. They were all younger than she was—Lina wasn't even eleven yet—but Tessa was going to think of being grown-up as her special thing until it didn't feel so special.

Tessa's teacher, Ms. Alfonso, was the first to notice how the boys all stared. She asked to see Mama at school, but Mama got mad and wouldn't talk about it. She called her *Miss* every time, emphasizing the last *s*, which teacher didn't like at all. Mama talked about Ms. Alfonso's *nerve* nonstop for two weeks, until Nana Pop, who almost never went out anymore because of her gout, caught Tessa playing spin the bottle with four boys in the weedy lot where she grew her tomato plants.

Tessa never meant to do wrong. She asked her brother's girlfriend Maura, who was always kissing Vinny, why she liked it so much, and Maura said, "Kissing all depends upon the boy," before Vinny came back and chased Tessa away.

She wanted to know more, so she told her nicest grown-up cousin, Nikki, what Maura had said. Nikki turned all wine-colored, but she couldn't hold her smile inside. "When you're ready, just make sure you kiss a boy you like."

Tessa was grown enough to be ready, but she didn't like one

particular boy. When the boys said they would fight over which of them could kiss her, Tessa suggested the bottle. That way the fighting was only a little bit of shoving, everyone got to stay friends, and Tessa had a chance to figure out what Maura meant. She only got to kiss Davey, and his lips were kind of wet. Maybe the tongue part would have been nicer, but Nana Pop scared him off with her cane before that happened.

Tessa was punished and stuck in her room until Mama said otherwise. Pop hit her three times with his belt, but only because Mama made him. Tessa saw how his face crinkled as he said, "Spin the bottle?" like he was more surprised than angry. Then Mama started going on about the house he had promised her, and that changed his mood real quick. The only one angrier than Mama was Vinny, because Mama wouldn't let Maura inside the apartment anymore. That meant they couldn't do any more deep kissing on the couch when she wasn't looking.

"Tessa, I have a job for you," Mama boomed from the kitchen. Tessa took one last look at her profile, shifting to her left side when her aunt crowded the doorway, steps ahead of Mama.

"Hello, my angel." Aunt Donna wrapped her in a protective hug, reached behind Tessa and hid the clothespin in her apron pocket.

"Angel?" Mama stood outside, as if Tessa's room was tainted by sin. "That's not the direction she's headed in. All the angels in Heaven are ashamed."

Tessa kissed her aunt's cheek. "Yes, Mama."

"Rae's dropping little Katie off for the night. You want to be kissing all the boys, you're going to get a dose of what that leads to. You'll be taking care of Katie till she leaves. That means watching, feeding, and cleaning up after her."

"Does kissing make babies?" Tessa had heard something about a *ragina* and *orgasms*, but nobody would tell her what that meant. Enza said she read some stuff in a book she didn't understand, but Tessa wasn't about to admit to her second-youngest cousin that she didn't know herself. She wanted to ask Maura, but Vinny would make sure that she never talked to Tessa again. Being the oldest of the youngest batch of cousins meant she got a whole lot of nothing all around.

"Never you mind about baby-making!" Mama roared. She pointed to Aunt Donna and said, "No feeling sorry for her. You make her work." Mama's finger turned Tessa's way. "If you watch any TV, Katie gets to choose. You think I get to watch what I want when you kids are around?"

Tessa nodded yes, although she didn't mean to.

"Rose Anna!" Aunt Donna's soft voice turned as loud as Mama's. "Children are a gift, not a punishment." She was shaking the way she did before she started the crying that took hours to stop.

"Of course they are, *cara*. I'm sorry. I'm sorry." Mama hugged Aunt Donna until her shaking stopped. Not even Mama could stand to see her cry that way, although nobody blamed Aunt Donna for being so sad. Two years after her youngest boy Jude was killed, her oldest went swimming drunk down at Coney Island and drowned. Now all she had was her daughter Rae and little Katie.

Tessa liked spending time with Katie. You could play with her like she was a doll, and she hardly ever cried. Not that Tessa was interested in playing with dolls now that she was almost thirteen.

"Ma-aaa?!" Rae called. Aunt Donna didn't look like she heard. Mama, Aunt Donna still in her arms, poked toward the hallway where Rae yelled twice more from the bottom floor. Tessa nodded at Mama and sighed. Tessa hoped she didn't have to entertain Rae very long. When Tessa was younger she had been her favorite babysitter, but Rae wasn't much fun now that she was grown.

"Hi," Tessa said when they converged on the stairs. Katie wasn't with her. Tessa looked down, and Katie was still a landing below them, making her way slowly up the stairs.

"Is she okay?" Tessa said. If Katie fell, Mama would blame her.

"She's not a baby," Rae said. "She has to learn."

"Mama wants me to watch her," Tessa said, bouncing down the stairs to Katie. Baby or not, she was still too small to reach the banister.

"I said *leave her*," Rae snapped. Tessa missed a step and had to grab on. Rae snorted, and Tessa looked back at her, then continued down the stairs to Katie. "Mama said for me to watch her."

"Did you leave that child alone on the stairs?" Mama asked. Tessa took the steps in leaps. She just hoped Katie could hold on till she got there, or she'd get the belt again for sure. "Girl if you were mine I'd take a strap to you this instant."

Mama's anger was directed in the right place for once. Tessa scooped Katie up and carried her past Rae, who was already heading down, ignoring Mama as she scolded, not stopping to say goodbye to Katie or waiting to see her own mother.

Tessa put Katie down safely past the top step, and Aunt Donna brightened as Katie squeezed through the door. "How's my precious baby?" She caught Katie in her arms and craned her neck past Tessa, looking for Rae. Katie kissed her Nana without saying hello.

"She left," Mama said gently. "She must have been running late."

Aunt Donna fumbled into the chair behind her. "Were you yelling?" she asked. As Katie settled into her lap, Aunt Donna's arms slowly dropped away. Tessa reached for Katie before Mama even pointed.

"It was nothing," Mama said. "Tessa was taking the steps too quickly."

Aunt Donna got up and left without answering, her body stiff and jerky like she wasn't fully awake.

Mama said, "There's no stopping the crying now." She stared at the door, mumbling, "Stupid, stupid girl."

"What should I do with Katie?" Tessa didn't like how Mama just stood there looking at the door.

"Katie can't see her that way. Keep her up here for now."

Mama let Lina and Franca come up, even though she was punished, because they wanted to play with Katie. "I'm babysitting, not playing," Tessa said, asserting her new authority.

"You can do both," Lina said.

"How would you know?" Tessa hated how Lina never seemed unsure. It made her impossible to boss around.

"My babysitters played with me," Lina insisted. "You should know, since you were usually there."

When Vinny or her older cousins used *How would you know?* on Tessa, she couldn't speak for hours from the shame. Tessa turned to Franca, "I suppose you want to play, too?" Tessa thought her tone was a bit like Mama's, and no one was more grown-up than her.

Franca shrugged. "What else is there to do?"

Katie had one shoe in her lap and was trying to tie the knot. Maybe she was bored, too. "What should we make her wear?" Tessa asked.

"What about this?" Lina held Tessa's other bra under her chin by the straps and put her fists in both cups so they poked out.

"Get off that!" Tessa's screech and lunge weren't very grown-up, but she blamed it on the company.

Franca laughed. "We'll get in trouble for sure."

"I'm in charge!" Tessa never understood why Lina and Franca had to be so close. Franca was *her* cousin, on her father's side. "This isn't a toy."

"What else is there to do?" They asked, in a unison that made Tessa's chest ache. Sometimes she hated every one of her relations.

"No!" Katie said, when Tessa tried to take her shirt off. It was her first word of the day.

Lina flopped on the floor next to Katie. "Why don't you want to play?"

"I play *shoe*," Katie said.

Tessa tossed her bra in Lina's lap. "Why don't you put it on? There wouldn't be any real difference."

Lina poked her fingers in the cups again. "I guess not." She took her shirt off and put her arms through the straps. She stood with her back to Tessa. "How do I do this?"

Tessa hooked it up, but the bra just drooped like Lina was the hanger it came on. "Needs some work," Tessa said.

"She needs socks," Franca said. Tessa pointed to her dresser, and Franca came back with both arms full.

"I don't think I need that many," Lina said. They all laughed so hard that Mama peeked in, and Lina had to dive behind the bed to keep from getting caught.

When Lina was stuffed, and she had admired herself in the mirror with her shirt on and off, Tessa said, "You're a good doll, too."

Katie said, "Me now!" and lifted her shirt. "Ouch!"

"Watch, your bandage is caught," Franca said, reaching to help her. "Tessa, come here."

"You can't get her shirt off?"

"Look!" Katie had a sore in the middle of her chest. It was covered with shiny stuff, but the wound was filmy and oozing green at the edges.

"Does it hurt?" Franca asked.

"Smoke," Katie said, with a nod.

"Mama," Tessa called. Lina shrieked and ran behind the bed to change.

"What?" Mama's hands were covered with flour.

Tessa pointed. "Her bandage came off and it looks real bad."

Mama wiped her hands on her apron and carried Katie to the kitchen, where the light was brightest. Mama was making cookies, even though Tessa was being punished. She hoped Mama would let her have one. "Katie, did you fall?"

"Smoke," Katie said, blowing bubbles with her tongue.

"Did she say *smoke*?"

Tessa nodded. "Before, too."

"Christ now, enough!" Mama said, and Tessa jumped back. "Not you. This came from a cigarette." Mama pulled a fresh spoon from the drainer and handed a scoop of dough to Tessa. "Just the one."

Mama paced a bit, Katie in her arms, while Tessa slowly licked cookie dough. "Go get your Uncle Pete right now." She nodded her head, caressed Katie's soft baby hair. "Let him be good for something today."

"But he's probably…" Tessa cut herself off, because the grown-ups never said *bar* out loud. "I don't want to go."

"Then get your brother to do it. Now."

"I'll go," Lina said, eyeing the cookie dough. Mama didn't offer her any, which was strange. Mama and the aunts were big on sharing. "My dad will be so relieved I'm not there for him that he'll probably shove Uncle Pete off his stool."

"Okay, you go then." Mama said. Franca waved and left with Lina, chewing on a fistful of hair.

"I'll kill him," Uncle Pete said. Katie fidgeted as he checked out her burn, then toddled straight back to Tessa when he let go. Tessa didn't blame her. Uncle Pete wasn't slurring, but Tessa could smell his breath from the kitchen. It wasn't just his breath, either. It was like he was sweating whiskey. She was glad Mama kept Pop from the bar. Most days, anyway. Pop had walked in with Uncle Pete, smelling like he did when he worked at the brewery.

"Send Vinny for him," Uncle Pete barked.

"Not my son," Mama said. Rae's husband, Sean, was a housing cop in South Brooklyn.

"Well, I can't send my own, now can I?" Despite his anger, Uncle Pete stood a step outside the kitchen, as if it was a threshold he wasn't allowed to cross.

"Getting my son killed in the projects won't bring yours back," Mama said, facing him down from the other side.

"Enough," Pop said, squeezing between them, a foot in each room. "I'll get him."

"Getting yourself—"

"Rose Anna, enough," Pop said. "Leave it to the men."

Mama snorted, but she didn't argue. She rolled up her sleeves and went back to her cookies, stopping only to point Tessa out of her kitchen.

Tessa took Katie by the hand. "Wanna watch some TV with me? I'll let you pick the channel."

They watched *Gilligan's Island* reruns, both half-sleeping on the floor until Pop returned alone. "He said it was an accident,"

Pop said to Mama right off. Uncle Pete was asleep at the table. Mama poked him with the handle of her wooden spoon, but he didn't wake up. She poked him a few more times, then slid a towel under him so he wouldn't drool on her good tablecloth.

Pop looked at Tessa, moved closer to Mama, and whispered, "He said he was worried about Rae, that he had his mother watching her now."

Mama looked at Tessa, who had climbed onto the closest chair, and was obviously listening. She shrugged. It wasn't her fault Pop had such a loud whisper. Mama pointed at Katie, but she was still watching TV, her head resting on Tessa's feet.

"I hope you washed them this morning," Mama said.

"It's not the top of my feet that get dirty." Tessa rarely sassed Mama, but she hated taking the blame for something so small in the middle of something big. If Rae hurt Katie, Tessa wanted her punished. She wanted her favorite aunt to stop crying, for everyone to stop making her feel bad. She wanted her father and her uncles to stop going to the bar, so Mama and the aunts would stop worrying. She wanted Mama to make it right no matter what because the whole family needed her to be that way, and because Tessa didn't want to be grown up in a world that made a woman like Mama look so afraid.

Mama sucked her lower lip between her teeth and nodded, as if she was having a conversation Tessa couldn't hear.

Pop said, "Do you believe it could be Rae?"

Mama rapped her knuckles against his skull. *"Stunad!* Who smokes?"

"I don't know." Pop swatted Mama's hand. "Girls don't hit."

Tessa cackled, then covered her mouth and looked down at Katie to avoid meeting her parents' eyes.

"Not my baby girl." Uncle Pete's fist hit the table. The noise twitched through Katie, who never looked away from the television. "Rae would never hurt anyone," Uncle Pete said. "Why didn't you bring him here, make him tell these lies to my face?"

"Man wears a gun," Pop said, with a shrug.

Uncle Pete pounded his chest, a gesture that only brought attention to its stoop. "I'll go get him myself." He looked at the floor as he sidestepped Mama.

Mama followed him. "Just a quick drink for courage, eh, Pete?" She nudged him with her elbow. "Shouldn't take more than two or three."

Uncle Pete waved her off, as the trembling in his hands creeped into his neck.

"Thanks for your help," Mama called down the stairs. "I'm so glad my sister married you for better or worse."

"You're the worse," Uncle Pete shouted back.

Mama turned right into Pop's folded arms. "You wanna talk for better or worse? You let me go—"

"*Leave it to the men,*" Mama mimicked.

Pop locked her chin in his hands, making Mama's face look small. "Have I wronged you, Rose Anna? Are a few beers on Saturday too much to ask?"

"They don't get us out of here any sooner." Mama's nails were deep in the flesh of his arm. Tessa wanted to yell at them both, scream how Katie didn't need to see them this way, but Katie's eyes were fixed on the evening news. Maybe it was smarter to look away and pretend there was nothing loud to overhear.

Pop squeezed Mama's chin toward Katie. "This one isn't even ours, and you're in the middle of it!" Pop let her go. "I don't believe you'd leave."

"We don't have to move far," Mama said. "But I want something ours and ours alone."

Tessa wasn't sure about moving. They had always lived here with the rest of Mama's family, with Pop's parents, Franca, and Uncle Mass across the street. As much as Lina and Enza and even Franca managed to annoy her every single day, she was grown enough to know being without them might be worse. Plus the boys here all noticed her now. Mama might be all hot to move just for that reason, but boys were probably the same all over Brooklyn.

Pop opened the door, and Tessa heard voices on the stairs. "There's a breeze. I'm going to sit on the stoop."

Mama sighed, and Pop said, "It'll happen, Rose Anna. You always get your way in the end."

Mama chewed her lip some more, and Tessa chewed her own lip, wondering what would happen between her parents. When she was younger and got punished, she imagined that Pop would come home from work and get so mad that he divorced Mama and took Tessa away to live with him alone. Then she would be close to him, like Franca was with her father. Now that Tessa was almost grown, she knew different. If she ever needed rescuing, it would come from Mama—flanked by the aunts—or not at all.

"Rae's coming up, and Donna's right behind her," Pop said, before the door shut.

Rae charged Mama. She smelled yeasty, like Pop. It wasn't a smell Tessa expected on a woman. "Who are you to butt into my life and cause trouble?"

"Rae!" Aunt Donna, close behind, said with a gasp. "Respect!"

"Who am I?" Mama repeated. She touched her chin, because Pop had hurt her or because she was thinking, Tessa couldn't tell. "I'm the one who held you while you cried through your entire baptism. I'm the one who gave you oatmeal baths and taped your fingers with gauze to protect that gorgeous complexion you have now when you gave your pregnant mother chicken pox, put her in the hospital, and caused the premature birth of your little brother, *God rest his soul.*" Mama walked arcs around Rae, her face scrunched in deep thought. "When you were old enough to know better, I carried you up the stairs, bathed you, and cleaned up your vomit when you decided to share a gallon of your Uncle Hugo's homemade wine with your friends. Is that enough? Can I ask about Katie now?"

Rae huffed and tapped, then turned mute. She pivoted as if she could hurl her words at Mama with the force of her hips and shoulders. When she failed again, Aunt Donna slapped her back, as if her voice was simply stuck behind a peanut or small fishbone.

"It was an accident," Aunt Donna said, finally speaking for her.

"She ran right into my cigarette." Rae sounded more like the girl she remembered, pleading with her to be good. "The kid never leaves me alone."

Tessa looked over at Katie sitting by the TV, quietly leaving everyone in the room, her mother included, alone. Mama said, "That child is clearly a handful."

"Rose Anna," Aunt Donna said, rubbing her temples. "She's upset enough. Don't make this worse than it has to be."

"Upset?" Mama said. "She's upset? According to your daughter, it's all Katie's fault. She deserves an infected burn for being so much trouble."

"Infected?" Aunt Donna turned to Rae. "How'd you let it get infected?"

"She's exaggerating."

"Show me!" Aunt Donna roared.

Mama nodded Tessa toward the kitchen. "Get Katie a cookie. They should be cool enough now. You can have one, too."

Katie chewed through her cookie quickly, ignoring Aunt Donna as she stripped off her top, removed the bandage, applied more antibiotic cream and another bandage, then kissed the top of her nose. When her cookie was gone, Katie plucked Tessa's from her fingers, giggling between greedy bites.

Tessa sighed, and Mama patted her shoulder. Maybe later Mama would let her have another, but she knew enough not to ask now.

Aunt Donna was quiet, her hands heavy on the armrest, her body in an awkward in-between position, as if she had started to sit and then changed her mind. "Where's her sweater? We're going to the emergency room right now."

"Don't overreact. I'll take her to the doctor on Monday, to make you feel better. Kids hurt themselves and then they heal."

"She's going to have a permanent scar!"

"You don't know—Katie, God damn it! Put that down now!"

Katie went into the kitchen for another cookie without Tessa noticing. She jumped at the sound of her mother's voice, and knocked the cookie sheet against the saucepan, which slid off the stove and splattered tomato sauce everywhere, including all over Katie.

"It wasn't cooked yet!" Mama said, as Aunt Donna screeched with Katie.

"Look what she did!" Rae said.

"What she did? You scared the pants off her!" Aunt Donna howled. "I'd wet myself if someone yelled at me like that!"

Mama tried to soothe Katie while she stretched for the dish towels in the pantry. "Run a bath," she told Tessa. The sauce on Katie's eyelashes accentuated how long they were, and Tessa bloated with guilt. It was her fault for not watching Katie, just because she was a little mad about her cookie.

As Tessa passed Mama, Katie caught a piece of her sweatshirt and wouldn't let go.

"See?" Rae said, "Like that. Every day like that!"

"What do you think you were like at her age? What the hell is wrong with you?" Aunt Donna said. "I didn't raise you this way. I'm ashamed. All the angels in Heaven are ashamed."

Mama handed Katie off, but Tessa looked long enough to show she knew exactly what problems Heaven's angels had to deal with.

Tessa brought Katie to the bathroom while Mama tried to get between Rae and Aunt Donna, who were nose-to-nose with the screaming and poking. Mama called for Aunt Alma, who lived across the hall, but she was probably in church, like always. Katie clung to Tessa's neck, her fingers pulling the fine hairs along her nape as she watched the tub fill. Tessa rubbed her back, but Katie kept on crying. Tessa tried hard not to think of all the snot and drool pouring out of Katie right now, which was mixing with the tomato sauce and leaving trails that looked like crusted blood on both of them.

Tessa poured shampoo in the tub and stirred the water with her foot, hitching Katie higher on her hip and wedging her shoulder into the wall to keep steady. Tessa had loved bubbles in her bath when she was small, and she hoped the sight of them would make Katie stop. The shampoo wasn't making the water very bubbly, Tessa's head was starting to throb with all the noise, and when she looked for Mama there were too many people in the way. Katie was so loud she hadn't noticed how the whole family had come either to watch or join the fight.

Lina came into the bathroom. "You're missing everything." She grimaced when Katie howled.

"Where's my mother?" Tessa asked.

"She's sitting on the top step, smoking two cigarettes at once."

"On purpose?"

Lina shrugged, peeked over Tessa's shoulder to get a better look at Katie. "Is she burned all over?"

"Huh? Just what you saw," Tessa said.

"What about when Rae threw the hot sauce all over her."

"It didn't happen that—" Aunt Alma poked her head inside the bathroom, and Lina had to sit on the toilet to make room.

Tessa held Katie out to her aunt, who said, "*Poverina*," and touched the cross of her rosary to Katie's hot forehead. Katie's fist connected, and the rosary fell into the tub. Aunt Alma said, "This is too hot for a baby," after she fished out her rosary. She toweled off the beads with the hem of her housedress. "Add some cold and then get her cleaned up."

"I don't know how to bathe her," Tessa said as Aunt Alma left.

"Just don't let her head go under," Lina offered.

"She won't stop crying!" Tessa held Katie out to Lina, who jumped off the toilet seat, her hands safely tucked under her arms.

"You're in charge," Lina said before leaving.

Tessa added cold water, then put Katie on the floor and stripped off her clothes. Katie didn't wear diapers anymore, but she needed one. Lina came in again, tripping on the towel Tessa had put along the door to try and muffle all the noise outside, hoping that would quiet Katie.

"Katie's other grandmother was here, and she left to call the cops! She kept saying we were all crazy, that her son married into crazy people. Then my Dad said that now even the dirty shanty Irish were putting on airs, so she called him a dumb Polack, and then he—"

"Shut up! I've got to calm her down!" Lina's eyes widened, but her mouth finally closed. She backed out, closing the door behind her.

Tessa put Katie in the tub, which made her scream louder. Both Tessa's sleeves were drenched, making her arms heavy. Tessa took her shirt off, trying not to think about what might get on her brand-new bra. She kept an eye on Katie when she had to let go, then used the cleanest of the dish towels to start wiping Katie down. The water was already red-tinged, so Tessa unplugged the drain. She added fresh water, making sure it never got too hot, then went back to cleaning Katie off.

As Katie got cleaner, she stopped struggling, and her cries turned to hiccoughs. Tessa did her best to soothe her, crooning, "It's okay. Mama loves you. Mama loves her baby girl." Her tone was meant to calm Katie, but the words kept Tessa steady when all she wanted was to dive right into her own Mama's arms. When she was finished with the bath, Tessa would edge Katie around all the craziness outside and try to find some quiet corner. Somewhere they could both just play.

Mayan Sunset

Maura sits atop the stone rail built to prevent guests from falling off the terrace and plunging into the rocks and water below. She's been warned all week to keep off, but from this perch she can still see the white speck of boat rocking and bobbing among the waves. Vinny said no to the kids' cruise, afraid they would miss their flight home, but Maura couldn't deny their daughter this final treat.

Maura ought to be inside packing, but she's hiding from Vinny's tight-lipped anger when he crosses *check on Ariana* from his list. Her stomach bubbles at the thought of another argument, but she breathes in air as deep and calming as the sea itself. She scrimped for this vacation for over a year, hiding half the Christmas money from Vinny, and withholding a portion of her waitress tips from the grocery fund. While it wasn't the trip she imagined, she regrets nothing. Maura has moved beyond her wistful couch-potato self, chain-watching the travel channel, compulsively paging through glossy-magazine fantasies on the supermarket-checkout line.

Maura tries to capture the view as the water ripples and changes shape below her. She has always lived near water—lakeside Chicago as a child; Pittsburgh, where three rivers converge, after her father died; then back to her mother's native Brooklyn along the East River, a place that looked as roughed-up as her mother had before she passed. That's where Maura met Vinny, sitting on an abandoned loading dock with his friends. She married him a few months after her mother died of breast cancer, when she was seventeen, pregnant, and still in high school. As the opening and closing of dresser drawers grates against the soothing rhythm of the surf, she wishes she could pinpoint exactly when she stopped feeling grateful.

❋

Vinny opened the door, put down their bags, and reached across the bed for the phone. Ariana ran arcs around the king-sized bed, and Maura peeked into the orderly, spacious bathroom. She wanted to point this out to Vinny, who believed indoor plumbing was exclusively American, but he had his back to her.

"Where do I sleep?" Ariana asked, and Maura showed her the door to the adjoining room. With Ariana distracted and Vinny occupied, she stepped onto the patio. They had argued over the price of the ocean view, but the water was a collage of blue, green, and purple, capped by rolls of foam raking the short sand beach.

Ariana ran out, banging her leg against the door she opened too quickly. "I have my own desk with a chair and there's paper with the hotel's name on it and it's fancy cause the letters are raised like you can trace them."

"You should write a letter to your grandparents before you leave."

"Daddy's on the phone with Gramma now."

"Again?"

Someone knocked, and Vinny yelled *Door* even though he was the only one inside. He offered her the phone as she passed. Her mother-in-law's voice echoed in the air, but Maura waved him off.

Ariana went back to circling the bed. Maura opened the door to a young woman with a clipboard and a sun-shaped name tag that covered half her chest. "I'm Staci Jones, I'm one of the counselors with the kid's club here. I just wanted to invite your—" Staci double-checked her clipboard, "—Adriana—"

"Ariana," Maura said.

"I'm sorry, Ariana." She made the correction with a pen that hung around her neck. "Anyway I just wanted to know if Ariana wanted to take trampoline lessons with the other children. We're starting in about twenty minutes."

Ariana darted toward her mother as soon as she heard her name. "I want to play on the trampoline." She tugged on her mother's arm as Maura bent down and asked, "What's a trampoline?"

Maura pushed her daughter's bangs out of her eyes. "Put your sneakers back on, you'll love it."

Staci handed Maura her clipboard. "I need you to sign a permission slip. Right by the X is fine."

"Ariana, Gramma wants to talk to you," Vinny said.

Maura handed the clipboard back to Staci. "She can't talk. She's got to leave right now to meet the other kids."

"What?" He tried to join them at the door, but the cord wouldn't reach. "I don't know, Ma, something about a trampoline…It's a bunch of kids together, how dangerous could it be?" He slowly stretched out the cord with his fingers. "Ma wants to talk to you."

Maura reached lazily for the phone and missed. The handset snapped back and ricocheted against the wall. Maura hurried Ariana out the door as Vinny retrieved the phone. "Hello, Ma. She'll be fine…No…No…Do I know how old—I had the front-row seat when she was born!" Maura rapped the handset against the wall. "Oops, door again. See you next week."

"You could have asked me about the trampoline," Vinny said.

"You called your mother as soon as we got off the plane."

"We talked five minutes!"

"Do you hear yourself?"

"We're in a whole different country!"

"Jesus, why'd you bother coming?" Maura bowled past him and shut the bathroom door. She sat on the edge of the tub and pulled at her braid. Maura wouldn't have survived her first two years of motherhood without Rose Anna as cheerleader and guide, but there were boundaries she respected with Ariana that seemed fused between her husband and his mother. She wanted a space in her life with Vinny where *la mamma* didn't reign. When Maura got pregnant, she agreed to move into the house his parents were buying because their share of the mortgage would help and still be cheaper than renting. But Maura didn't want to spend the rest of her life in a basement. "Just another year or two," he kept saying.

There was a gentle knock at the door, which she pretended not to hear. "I'm sorry. I don't want to start out like this," Vinny said through the door.

Maura unlocked the door, and he swung her by the waist until she had to hold on for balance. Just as her mood began to lift, he said, "I know it's hard for you to understand, but if your parents were still around you'd do the same things."

Maura didn't think she would, but then she couldn't say for sure.

❈

Maura nudged the lump underneath the covers, but Vinny wouldn't stir. She pushed with both hands, rocking him. Last night, they had put Ariana to bed and splurged on paella and a flamenco show, followed by hours of dancing where Vinny had shown off the *salsa* skills he had picked up as a neighborhood boy. But she had been up with Ariana since sunrise, energized by the sight of an orange splash rising up from the sea.

"Help me."

Ariana bounced up and down on the bed, showing off her trampoline skills, but he rolled over and stuffed his head under a pillow.

"Vinny, we only have one week here," Maura pleaded, sounding like her daughter at bedtime.

Ariana flopped onto the bed and ducked her head under her father's pillow. Maura heard loud smooch noises mixed with her daughter's giggles. Maura crouched for a better look as Vinny turned away and could see him trying not to smile. She thought her daughter had an instinct for making the right gesture, a quality Maura admired and sometimes envied. She dropped down on Vinny's other side to pen him in, and Vinny's arm came up around her as she nibbled at and giggled into his ear. They laughed and rolled together, lapping up the sun that never reached their dreary home. Maura thought it was a perfect family moment, containing all and only them.

After breakfast they took the bus into Cancún City to visit the marketplace. "They don't drive as badly here as I thought they would," Vinny said, as he looked at the passing traffic. Ariana left the seat by her mother and crossed over to her father's lap. She pressed up against the glass as she looked out the hazy window. "Get your face off there, you don't know where it's been," he said.

Maura said, "We could rent a car tomorrow and go exploring on our own. Visit some of the Mayan ruins along the way, see native villages, have a picnic and—"

"Enough with the guidebook!" He pulled at Ariana's ponytail, and she moved her face off the dirty glass. "Don't you want to relax?"

"I want to do things."

Several people got off, so Vinny stretched himself across the seat, sponging up the excess space. Ariana's face was mashed up against the glass again, so he pulled her away, making her sit properly, his arm around her to curb her fidgeting. "Well, the only thing I'm exploring tomorrow is the pool with the floating bar."

"Then we'll just go without you," Maura said.

Vinny's arms tightened, and Ariana squirmed away and crossed to her mother, where she looked out the other window. "I'm not letting you take her into the middle of a strange country by yourself."

"There it is, Kiwi Marketplace. Let's go." Maura took Ariana's hand and exited through the rear. They crossed the boulevard without waiting for him, but he caught up on the other side. His hand was pressed against his forehead. "I was right behind you, you let the door snap back in my face."

"I was helping her down the steps." Maura peeled his hand away. "You don't even have a mark."

Vinny spun around in a tight little circle. "What did I do now?"

"I hate it when you tell me what to do!"

"You want to go off all by yourself, be my guest." He backed away from her, jerking his thumb in her direction and telling pass-ersby, "My wife, Ponce de León."

Maura walked off in the opposite direction, pulling a reluctant Ariana along with her. "Why are we leaving Daddy?"

"Girl time." Maura couldn't keep the sharpness from her voice. Vinny acted like he was her father, and that was no way for a grown woman to live. He took the fun out of shopping, always barking directions. *Don't spend too much money. Don't stand there and let that man flirt with you. Hold your purse more securely.* She was happy to be rid of him.

The marketplace was a large collection of individual mer-chants' tents, each trying to outshine the other with outrageous splashes of color, beginning on the boulevard and sprawling back-ward onto the beach. The merchants themselves were shouting things like *Orgy, Freebies,* and *Come see my junk,* in order to attract tourists like herself. She bought a russet-stained straw hat, almost the same shade as her hair, for herself from one merchant and a sun-dyed dress, called a *huipil,* for Ariana from another.

Maura needed a gift for her mother-in-law, something so perfect Rose Anna wouldn't frown at her, question her about the price, or immediately tick off five ways the money might have been better spent. At her side, Ariana kept scanning the crowd for Vinny, although she stopped searching whenever Maura caught her eye. Maura settled on a loosely woven ta-blecloth, shimmery beige trimmed with a bold Aztec pattern in reds and golds. She haggled the merchant down to nearly half his original price, then slowly counted out the unfamiliar bills.

When she had the tablecloth folded into her bag, she reached for Ariana's hand, but she was no longer at her side.

Maura called out her name, trying to push away the crowd that obscured her view. She ran in any direction that offered more space or a vista, calling, *Ariana, Ariana.* As Maura searched, her mind played kidnapping scenarios that made her throat burn. She switched directions too often to maintain her bearings, then broke free of the maze into an area of the beach littered with half-demolished tents. All she could see was the water and the labyrinth of the market.

She turned again and walked into a group of men sitting in the sand, drinking from a jug they passed around. She ran up to them. "Have you seen my daughter? A little girl, long legs, brown hair in a ponytail?"

A man appeared by her shoulder, and touched her hair. "Roja, linda," he said.

Maura jerked away from him. "I need to find my daughter. If you haven't seen her, can you tell me how to get back onto the boulevard?"

The man grabbed her arm and said, "I take you." He started leading her toward the water, but she locked her knees and refused to move. He was barrel-shaped, balanced on short, compact legs. Alone, he was hardly a threat, but his friends were starting to rise to their feet. She twisted free with a kick and ran back into the maze of tents.

Maura tried to focus on her breathing. She couldn't help her daughter without a clear head, but she pictured those men touching Ariana's hair and pulling her toward the water, and her rasping quickened. She wailed for Vinny. He would know exactly how to find Ariana. He would never have lost her or gotten lost. If she found Vinny, Ariana would be fine.

She walked on, twitching from the need to split apart and search every alley, in all directions, at once. She called for them both, alternating their names, until she overheard, "*Señor,* over here. I see her, red hair, *bonita.*"

She turned and saw Vinny walking toward her, Ariana lagging behind him. She ran and scooped up her daughter. "I don't think I've ever been so scared."

"I knew you'd be crazed." He massaged her shoulder. "We've been looking all over for you."

She shook Ariana. "Don't ever leave me." Ariana buried her head in Maura's chest and cried.

"I've already given her hell. She saw me across the crowd..." Vinny took Maura's packages and draped his arm across her shoulders. "Everything's okay. Let's take a taxi back to the hotel. Nothing bad happened, hon...you need to calm down."

As they rode back, Maura wanted nothing better than to calm herself, but she couldn't shake the anxiety that rippled up and down her spine, scenes of what-could-have-been still unfolding in her head.

❊

Maura and Vinny were tucked inside a large, porous piece of coral perched upon a cliff's edge. They were in the ruins of the ancient city of Tulum, waiting for the sun to set over a stone temple and sink into the sea below. It was a couples' tour called Mayan Sunset. Of course, Ariana refused to stay behind, but she was enjoying a squealing game of tag with some other children.

Vinny's hands roamed inside the bell of her dress, his touch light and easy. She'd forgotten how slow and soft he could be. They had more sex than most married couples, but it was done with an eye toward the clock, a release that eased them into a sleep that was always too short. Years of *getting on with it* made her sigh from the toes she'd just been flexing.

Vinny squeezed her fingers. "I'm going to miss looking at water that's really blue, not dirty-dishwater gray."

"Well, then...maybe it's time for us to dump that dishwater."

Vinny snorted. "What? Dredge the river and refill it with some magic vial an old Mexican shopkeeper sold you?"

"There are places with clean rivers—cleaner rivers, anyway—and cleaner air, too."

Vinny's hands stopped, and she tried to prod them back to work. "I guess we weren't born lucky."

"We're not tithed to the land, Vin," Maura said. "How long can you let your child live without windows?"

"You're exaggerating." He shrugged her off and hugged his legs against his chest. "We have a good life. I don't know why you can't see that."

Maura was certain theirs wasn't a *good* life, but she could imagine having less. "Vinny, are you *really* happy?"

"I'm," he paused, "content." He smiled as if he made the perfect choice. Maura put her head down, and he pressed on. "I can't leave my family. You have to forget these wild ideas."

"Ariana and I are your family!"

Vinny swiveled toward Ariana's exuberant laughter. "She's being really loud."

He pushed himself up, but Maura reached for his hand. "Leave her alone. How often does she get to be so free?"

Vinny kicked at the ground, and stones skidded over the edge. "We might not live someplace fancy, but it's where our parents were born and I was born and our kid was born and that should count for something."

"Sunlight counts more." Maura tidied the sand he'd disturbed. "I'm tired of feeling like a half-dead plant."

Vinny took hold of Maura's wrist and pointed her arm toward Ariana. "Look how close she's running to the edge."

Maura wrenched free. "What are you going to do when she's a teenager? Let the child have some fucking fun!" The intensity of her own voice startled her, and as Maura looked around in the semi-darkness at the people moving about, she realized they had missed the sunset.

❀

Maura tried to focus on the horizon, willing herself to ignore the nausea as the ferry from Isla de las Mujeres raced and rocked across the sea. She could feel the tension in Vinny where their bodies were forced to touch by the lurching motion of the boat. For the past two days they had spoken only when necessary. She looked at the other passengers, willing herself to concentrate on anything except the rickety construction of the boat. Ariana and a girl about ten were the only things in constant motion, picking up stray cups and making trips to the garbage can inside the cabin. Maura admired their energy, which contrasted with the lethargy of all the adults who seemed depleted either by seasickness or the complimentary alcohol.

Vinny said, "What is she doing with that girl?"

"They're cleaning up."

"Call her over."

"Why?"

"Ariana, come over here now!"

"What are you doing?" Maura said.

"Something's not right."

Ariana ran to her father and jumped into his lap. She kissed him loudly on the cheek and said, "I hate it when you and Mommy fight."

Vinny plopped her onto Maura's lap. "Smell her breath."

Maura couldn't smell anything, but Ariana's eyes looked unfocused. "Sweetie, did you drink from those cups you were picking up?"

"Just a couple of sips. Kelly dared me to."

Vinny tapped her shoulder and pointed. "I think Kelly over there had more than a few sips."

Kelly slouched at a woman's feet, vomiting. The woman said, "This time, you'll learn the hard way." She picked up her towel and her drink and casually strolled into the cabin.

Maura tried to gauge her daughter's condition. "You don't feel funny, do you?"

"Am I in trouble?" Ariana asked.

Vinny said, "Look at your friend over there. What do you

think?" But his voice softened as he muttered *ignorant bitch* under his breath. "You watch her."

Vinny walked over to the crying, vomiting girl. Several passengers hovered around her, saying things like, "You okay, honey?" when she obviously wasn't. Vinny carried her over to the rail, smoothed the hair from her face, and stayed with her until the spasms stopped. Then he sat her down and cleaned her up, stripping her down to her swimsuit and giving her his own shirt to wear. He made use of the onlookers by recruiting them to fetch juice and pills for seasickness. Even after the crowd diminished and her mother returned, Vinny stayed with her, helping her breathe and focus on the horizon while Maura watched, clutching their child tightly in her arms.

✺

"If you slip off that rail, there's not much I could do to rescue you."

His voice startles her, but Maura maintains her balance. He's leaning against the door. She wipes the tears from her eyes, and carefully steps back onto the terrace. "I don't need to be rescued."

"You will." Vinny traces a path down her nose with his finger. "Sooner or later." Maura steps back, separates herself from his touch. She fears the truth in his words even as they make her angry. "When were you planning to tell me she was gone?"

"I figured you'd notice eventually."

"It's crazy, after what happened," Vinny said.

Maura squeezes the rail, tries to steady her mind. "That's why I let her go, so she knows we trust her not to make the same mistakes."

"What if she screws up again?"

"Then I guess that's something we should know about her sooner rather than later, don't you think?"

Vinny kicks the café chair. "I'm so sick of your nutso parenting ideas."

He doesn't trust her. This is why they will never move from his parents' basement. "I'm sick of living underground."

Vinny cocks his head slightly, raises his right eyebrow and says, "Do you want her to grow up fatherless and end up just like you?"

Maura flinches, just as she is supposed to. "If I'm such a terrible example, why did you marry me?"

Vinny, hands clasped behind his back, paces in short military steps. His words adopt the rhythm of his body. "You think you know yourself, but you don't. You want to believe that you're brave and adventurous, but you're not. You're the most skittish person I've ever known. You'd run from your own shadow if it came too close."

Every word punctures her courage. She turns away, toward the water. "Ariana and I are moving with or without you."

He laughs, but it sounds as if he's out of breath. "This place just has you all worked up." She feels his hands on her shoulders, rubbing at the tension she intends to keep. "Let's get Ariana. It's time to leave."

He kisses her, and she feels the rough stab of stubble against her cheek. She closes her eyes tightly and the colors below transfer to her eyelids. "I know it's time," she answers, but he's already gone inside.

Make Your Wedding *Perfect!*

The most important decision you make may be your dress. The bridal gown sets the tone for the entire wedding. Choose carefully, brides!

*Y*ou've got to stop dieting. You can't be a beautiful bride if your dress fits like a potato sack." Aggie pinched the new seam roughly, catching Lina's skin. She stamped her foot, sending loose pins rolling off the table. Lina's six bridesmaids scrambled after them with dog-like obedience, crawling across the floor in their mauve-colored slips. This was supposed to be their fitting, before Aggie had bet her seamstress fee that Lina had lost more weight and needed to be refitted. Again. Another eight pounds, after she reached her goal weight two months ago. Lina was told to think of every quarter pound as a stick of butter, and she imagined another thirty-two sticks trailing after her like a makeshift train, dissolving into pools of grease as she walked down the aisle.

Lina's wedding dress was a reproduction of a flapper dress from the twenties, in an aged-antique color that was, according to her mother, "Too far from white." It was a shift style but not form-less. She found it tucked in the back pages of a bridal magazine. In the picture, the dress hugged the model's curves in a way that whispered rather than hooted. On Lina, the sample gown looked much less fluid, but she had been determined to change her body, not the dress.

Her bridesmaids made the right cooing noises, praised her for her *bold choice* and gulped back questions about the dresses they'd be wearing.

When Lina's mother saw the dress, she said, "If you wear that, I won't come."

Lina said, "I understand," and thrust her credit card at the clerk. She didn't believe her mother. Her sister Nikki had eloped, so this was her only opportunity to play mother-of-the-bride.

What Lina most loved about the dress was the expression on the model's face in the picture she saw. Her head was tilted slightly upwards, eyelids at half-mast, complexion shining as if lit from within by candlelight. The model seemed caught in some perfect moment of interior joy. Lina had believed she would exude this ecstatic certainty, carry it with her down the aisle and into the ever after of her marriage when the dress fit her the way it fit the model. When she met her goal weight, the dress had fit exactly as she imagined. As Lina twirled, the silky fringe wrapped her in a circle of motion. Her curves had sharpened, and her silhouette was elegant from every angle. She exuded ecstasy, if not certainty.

But that moment had already come and gone.

The proposal is the first official wedding act, and as such, is a moment that will be asked about and retold throughout the years of your marriage. Do you want this story to be a dull and ordinary one? Is that any way to begin a life with your beloved?

Jack was acting strangely. Tickets to *Les Misérables*, which his own sister had seen for her anniversary and called, "The musical version of a chick flick." Dinner at one of the city's most romantic restaurants, straight from an article she had tacked to her fridge last year. "Spur-of-the-moment," he said, when he hated doing things last minute. He never once cursed the midtown traffic, never flinched at the pre-theatre prices posted on the wall of the parking garage. He looked so confined by the suit he bought for his sister's wedding, only two years old but already too tight across the shoulders and chest.

The waiter brought a single red rose to the table. Jack tickled her nose with it.

"Just tell me the bad news." Lina was sure he'd been laid off, and he wanted the memory of this splurge to last through the long months of video rentals and aimless walks through the neighborhood.

"Bad news?" Jack's eyebrows jutted into V formation. "We're celebrating."

"Celebrating what?" Lina asked.

"Being in love." He handed her the rose and cupped her fingers around the bud.

Celebrating love? She dropped the rose onto her plate and watched him watch her. "What are you up to?" Was he cheating? He didn't look caught in a lie. He had that gooney grin she first saw back in junior high, when he took a week-long beating from the other boys for bringing daisies to school on Valentine's Day.

Jack motioned toward the rose with his wine glass. "Will you just please look at it?"

"It's not from you," she said.

He picked it up again, brought the bud to his nose. "Look closer!"

Lina leaned in, searching for some weird flaw. Jack loved pointing out oddities. She shrugged.

"Take it."

Lina plucked a petal. "He loves me," plucked another, "He loves me not."

"One more," he said.

"Why?"

He plucked a petal and tossed it in her direction. "Because I do love you." He slipped from his chair, onto his knees, digging his finger into the bud. Lina didn't catch on until the ring appeared, trailing more petals.

It was his grandmother's ring, a square and chunky setting with a dark yellow-gold band. Lina would be a younger bride than Nikki, who'd been twenty-two when she married Henry, wooed by a weekend in the Catskills spent ordering room service from a suite with a heart-shaped bed and jacuzzi.

Lina held out her palm, and Jack handed the ring to her, his lips quivering between outrage and amusement. She wanted to feel the weight before he put it on her finger. When she looked up, his face had gone still, as if freeing her to disappoint him. In kindergarten, he told her she shouldn't play Cat Woman because Batman would never marry a criminal. She could imagine telling that story to their children. She could imagine the children; a girl with Jack's dimpled smile and a mischievous boy with dirt-smudged cheeks.

She offered the ring back to him, and he slipped it onto her finger. The wedding march played over the sound system as the waiter brought champagne, holding the bottle high above him as he came to the table. The entire restaurant began to cheer. They toasted each other, sipping slowly from the tall crystal flutes, but Lina was pulled from the moment by the other diners, whose gawks and whispers scrutinized their lifetime-happiness potential.

Brides, don't be thrown off by wedding jitters. They are a natural re-action to this dramatic, life-changing event. Discuss your fears with friends and family, if necessary, and accept their assurances. Cold feet are so common they should be on your checklist!

Lina's sister Nikki, who was seven months pregnant by her mystery guy, had been banned from the wedding by maternal decree. Nikki was the more obedient child and refused Lina's request to ignore their mother. Nikki promised, barring labor, to watch Lina get married from the back row of the church. Nikki knew Lina hated to lose an argument, even by default, and was making the wedding favors—mauve-lace pouches of Jordan almonds and a heart-shaped pin with a mauve ribbon that said *Jack & Lina to-gether forever*—to atone.

"Why did you marry Henry?" Lina asked, as she watched Nikki make perfect glue trails. Nikki wouldn't let her help. The kids were with her ex-husband's parents for the night, and that was *help enough* for her sister.

"He asked me," Nikki said without bitterness or nostalgia. Henry left her with three children under five to raise alone.

"Because he asked you? That's your reason?" Lina didn't know why her tone was so sharp. She had heard worse.

"He always smelled nice," Nikki said, with a smirk. "And he was the first man I met who hated the taste of alcohol. I thought that boded well for fatherhood."

"Did you love him?"

"Maybe it's different with you and Jack, because you're the girl he always wanted." Nikki picked up the ribbon she was about to glue, as if reading the message for the first time. "I know he's good to you, and I hope he stays that way. But we'll just raise our kids together if he doesn't. Like Mom and the aunts, only without all the nonsense they tolerated because of that *divorce is a mortal sin* bullshit."

Lina stared, an old habit she had mostly left behind. "You wanted her to kick Pop out?"

"I'd have packed his bags and called the cab." Nikki shifted in her chair, adding a pillow to support her middle back, and went back to gluing *Jack & Lina together forever* ribbons to white plastic hearts.

A married couple's first home is the physical embodiment of their relationship. It should represent neither the bride nor the groom's individual tastes, but their shared sensibilities. Brides, don't neglect your groom's tastes and needs!

"Exit 66, a quarter of a mile," Lina adjusted the shoulder strap where it rubbed her underarm. She hated long car rides. With traffic, this one was well over two hours old.

"The traffic won't always be this bad," Jack said.

"It's Sunday morning. This is probably as good as it gets."

"That can't be true." Jack's voice lacked authority. The Long Island Expressway was notorious for traffic jams.

"We don't need four bedrooms." Lina didn't want to live in Suffolk County.

"It's in our price range." Jack didn't slow down as the exit curved, and her stomach lurched with the sudden shifts in direction.

"It's in the boonies," she said, although the street they were driving on wasn't much different from the other streets they'd looked at, closer to the city.

Jack pointed out a construction site that looked like a half-built strip mall. "We could both get jobs out here."

"I like the job I have." The building was a stucco rectangle with green-tinted glass. Jack's company renovated landmark buildings in the city. This pre-fab construction wasn't the right kind of work for a craftsman. Why couldn't Jack see he'd be unhappy?

"No, you don't," he said.

Lina was a customer service representative at HBO. It wasn't the kind of job you liked, but she was lucky to have it. They generally hired college grads, and it paid as well as construction. She was the only neighborhood girl she knew with her own apartment. "Well, the people are cool. I don't want to switch."

"And I thought you were the adventurous one." He pointed out another building site, but she looked out the back window instead, toward home.

"Moving to the suburbs is no adventure." It came out shrill, but Jack didn't seem to mind.

"What do you see?" he asked, as they turned off the main road.

This street was residential. The houses seemed to come in four basic styles. The landscaping was identical—lawn, border hedge, tree. *The Twilight Zone.*

"What's wrong with this?" Jack rolled down his window. "It smells nice. Like nature."

The cold wind raised the hair on her arms. "It's creepy."

Jack slowed down to cross train tracks. "You want to live in an apartment your whole life?"

"What's better about this, exactly?" She knew what they were supposed to think, but—as usual—couldn't wrap her own ideas around the prevailing view. Maybe it would be nice to have a house, but being out here reminded her of the yearly visits to her grandparents' graves, with everything within sight neatly arranged and manicured.

"Fuck, Lina. We're getting married." His fingers strummed the steering wheel and accidentally sounded the horn. "Where do you want to live?"

Lina's street had three restaurants that she liked, and even Jack admitted the pizza place a few blocks down was *Brooklyn* good. "You already live with me most of the time."

"Your apartment's too small."

Jack pulled the car into a driveway. There was a minivan in front of them. If they moved here, how many years before Jack drove one of those monsters off a car lot? "I don't want our kids to grow up in the city."

"We don't have kids!" Lina said. Jack unbuckled his seat belt, and opened the door. "Please don't. I don't want to live here."

"What?" He looked over at the realtor, a rumpled blonde having a smoke, and lowered his voice. "We just spent two and half hours getting here."

Lina thought the ding ding ding of the car-door reminder might actually drive her mad. "If you love me, you'll shut the door and drive away."

Jack got out and walked over to the realtor. Lina didn't budge. She watched him talk to the woman, shake her hand, then slowly return to the car. As he backed out of the driveway, he said, "We're stopping to eat on the way home, and you're not having any of that leafy salad shit. This diet's making you fucking fruit loops."

Writing your own vows makes your wedding ceremony personal and unique, just like your love and the course of your future life together. Sharpen those pencils, brides and grooms!

Lina wrote *You are my truest friend* and *I take you as my husband* and crossed it out. Wedding vows were supposed to be more romantic, more dripping with gooey love. Jack was in her kitchen.

He had moved her table to the wall, and left her toaster, radio, and box of Cheerios sitting in the middle of the floor where it used to be. Now his nose nearly touched the notepad as he wrote. And wrote. He didn't seem to have any trouble making himself comfortable or getting his thoughts on paper.

Lina chewed through three pencils in the next hour. She had eraser shavings all over her tongue, and her breath smelled like synthetic rubber. She had rewritten *You are my truest friend* seven times on three different sheets of paper. Lina was stumped. How do you write gooey love for someone who let you pretend his G.I. Joe was really Ken on a date with Barbie? Gooey love was fleeting, one-dimensional. She and Jack already shared their lives. Getting married only acknowledged what already was between them.

"Want to hear mine?" he asked from the kitchen. He was beside her before she had time to answer.

"Okay." She turned her paper over so he couldn't see what she'd written.

"I take you as my wife because my life begins and ends with you. Your love fills me up and makes me stronger. I want you as my wife because the story of our life has always been love."

Gooey love extravaganza! His hair stuck out on his left side, from leaning against the wall. Jack had never seemed so flawed, yet so perfect.

"What do you think?" he asked, but Lina didn't want to think.

"Let's both use yours." She steered him to the bedroom by his belt loops in order to end the conversation.

A bridal shower honors the bride and allows her friends and family to celebrate her good fortune, as is fitting, with attention and gifts. Prepare to be surprised, brides, unless you want to be immortalized wearing sweatpants and a hat made of bows and ribbon!

"Come on," Franca, her maid-of-honor, said as Lina went back inside her building to fetch her purse. "They won't keep the table if we're late."

It was today. Lina knew it, and she double-checked her make-up in the bathroom mirror. A bit too soon, but Franca was a fidgety liar. Lina ran down all three flights, eager for the tribute to begin.

Lina's bridesmaids, who seemed to move as one now, led her to a chair on a dais decorated with mauve crêpe paper. "It's a blessings shower!" they told her, then proceeded, one-by-one throughout the room until everyone had spoken, to recite bits of poetic advice and prayers to support the union of her soul with Jack's. Theirs should be a fertile garden of love, but their togetherness should have space within it and God, who created this bond, would protect it for the price of a mere prayer. Or maybe it was the garden that needed space. Or God. Lina didn't have to worry, because these precious blessings were copied down in calligraphy on small squares of thick parchment—also mauve—and pinned to a wrap that was not-quite-mauve in this light, which they draped around her delicate bride shoulders.

Franca stood over her and joined the two ends so it wouldn't slip off. "It's not much, but I convinced them that making you wear the bow hat would detract from the sanctity of wearing your loved ones' blessings." Lina clutched her hand before she moved away. Ever practical, Franca was somehow immune from the hive mind.

Lina was grateful when a present was placed in her lap and she was commanded to let rip. Her mother's family, who lacked money but not numbers, had banded together in groups of three to six to buy presents, mostly china and silverware, each group buying a piece of the set until she had the means to throw a feast in their honor. This coordinated effort was the conversational buzz of her shower.

The parade of gifts was long and exhausting, with no food break for the bride. The great unveiling wasn't as exciting as she'd imagined. Lina didn't have room for an industrial-sized blender or a canister vacuum a child could ride. These gifts said, *All your family and friends support Jack's plan to buy that house in the burbs*, in a neighborhood that wasn't walking distance from work, where the commuter rail pass cost a lot more than a subway token.

When she argued with Jack about the wedding, even her future mother-in-law agreed, "This is the bride's day." It was such a magical phrase. She wished it could transfer into other areas of her life, like on the phone with a customer at work or waiting in the token line on Monday mornings along with every other loser who forgot to plan ahead.

But the bride magic was waning. Now that they were planning their lives, shifting from *getting* to *being* married, she heard, "You must learn to bend. No marriage can succeed without sacrifice," from every woman she knew. Did the men in Jack's life give him the same advice? Lina wasn't hopeful. As she was kissed and cuddled by all her female friends and relatives, her bridesmaids staunchly protecting the blessings cape still draped across her shoulders, she wondered if all this frilly wedding fanfare merely camouflaged the hard sell of a one-sided contract.

Brides, don't be thrown off by wedding jitters. They are a natural reaction to this dramatic, life-changing event. A romantic evening with your partner (sans wedding details) is usually a quick and easy cure.

Jack cancelled the night Lina's mother cooked dinner to celebrate the booking of the wedding hall. Her mother still made red peppers stuffed with sausage and tortellini fra diavolo, Jack's favorites, rather than Lina's grilled eggplant or cheese ravioli. Perhaps she was annoyed with both of them when, after all but their coffee cups had been cleared and washed, she said, "I'm not sure I want to get married."

"What happened?" Her mother put her cup down, and her fingers immediately went into overdrive massaging her knuckles. All the women in Lina's family worried through their hands. "Did Jack lose his job?"

"No," Lina said. "He's still working steady."

Her mother shook her head. "He's hit you." She pushed the

saucer as far as her arm could reach. "If he hits before the wedding, he'll hit the children, too."

"Jack has never hit me." Lina pushed her own cup away and stilled her hands only when she noticed the similarity.

"He didn't hit you?" Her mother looked doubtful, as if Lina had confessed and then recanted.

"No," she snapped. "Come on, you've known him his whole life."

"Oh, Lina." Her mother took the coffee cup poised at Lina's chin and walked it to the sink. "You can't get me worked up like you used to. I'm too old now."

Lina followed her mother. "So if Jack has a job and doesn't hit me, I should consider myself lucky?"

"Look around you." Her mother gyrated the soap brush like a mad compass needle. "In our world, that's gold. Why must you always be so far away, so far above? What good will come of that the day you need us or we need you?"

Lina's head slumped, and her mother shooed her back to the table. She handed Lina the red-velvet roller and thumped her fingers on the tablecloth. Her mother sat to finish the last of her coffee, sighing between sips as she pointed out stray crumbs.

For many couples, a wedding is a sacred ritual as well as an event. Catholic pre-marriage counseling, or Pre-Cana, provides spiritual guidance for a couple as they join together. Remember your priorities, brides—a lovely wedding will last a day, but a loving marriage is for life!

Lina sat patiently in her gray folding chair and listened to a celibate man discuss sex. "God's love is passionate, and he wants you to take the ecstasy you feel when you're close to Him and share it with each other," Father Peralta said.

Jack shifted forward in his chair. "Oh, yes, Father. We want that, too."

"You are both children of this parish, so I know you've waited for God to bless this union."

Lina was silent. Jack said, "Of course, Father."

"We have sex." Lina was unprepared for her own honesty, but she liked it. Her spine backed into the chair, stretched taller.

"Yes, but it was a choice we really struggled with." Jack crossed himself twice. Once for each lie.

Father Peralta nodded slowly, patting the Bible he held in his hand. He was about to speak when Lina cut him off. "We had sex in a car on our second date and we weren't virgins then either."

Jack folded his hands over his face, as if in prayer. "You're making a liar out of me."

"How did I make you lie, exactly?" Lina asked.

"Jack, perhaps we need to discuss why you felt the need to hide these truths from me," Father Peralta said. "The Lord, of course, knows."

"Lina's not sure she believes in God anymore," Jack blurted.

Father Peralta raised his left eyebrow, slowly shifting his glance her way. "Lina?"

She shrugged. "I'm the truthful one."

"Are you here because you want God's approval to enter the sacrament of marriage?"

"Not really," she said, resorting to the shrug again. "I'm here because Jack really wanted to get married in church and I figured that would be okay." She paused, then cut off Father Peralta again. "My family expects it, too, so I'm trying to rise above my personal doubts for my loved ones."

Father Peralta raised his bible, and Lina thumped its cover. "Jesus is big on tolerance, no?"

Father Peralta's lips parted again. When his pause went uninterrupted, he said, "What do you think of that, Jack?"

"I think she's a bad Catholic." Jack's lower lip trembled, recreating a stutter he had left behind in grade school. Lina reached for Jack's hand, which he snatched away and then repented. It meant so much to have known Jack so long and so well that she held on and listened without comment as Father Peralta sidestepped her doubts and lectured on the difference between following the letter and the spirit of God's law.

Brides, don't be thrown off by wedding jitters. They are a natural reaction to this dramatic, life-changing event. When doubts seem particularly stressful, try to imagine life without your beloved. Now doesn't that just work wonders for your perspective?

"I'm going to miss this," Franca said from the pile of pillows Lina kept near the TV, discards from Nikki's embroidered crafts phase.

"Why don't you take over my lease?" Lina had renewed last month, increasing the tension between her and Jack.

"You'd actually have to move first." Franca squealed as she found *Captain Blood* on the classics channel. Franca grew up playing cards and watching old movies with her grandparents.

"I found this company called Air Hitch," Lina said. "You pay them $150 and they promise to get you on a plane to somewhere in Europe within three days. Doesn't that sound so much more exciting than some honeymoon-with-other-honeymooners package?"

The pirate and his beautiful hostage were arguing, nose to nose. Franca muted the sound. "Are you sure about getting married?"

"Why?" Lina asked, distracted. Her attention had drifted to the impending onscreen kiss.

Franca pointed at the screen. "Fighting is great for movie romance, but—"

"Jack is the kind of guy you marry, right?"

"He's definitely a catch." Franca's nod swayed into a headshake. "I want a house, someplace with grass, where you can't hear your neighbors in the bathroom."

"You'd never leave your Dad or the grands." Lina lunged for the remote, but Franca tossed it into the pillow pile.

"They'd follow me anywhere, but I wouldn't let them come on my fancy Jamaican honeymoon."

"I don't want one of those stuff-your-face and get-sloshed-by-the-pool trips."

"Jack thinks that's honeymoon nirvana!" Franca stormed the TV, poking the off button. "Jack thinks Long Island is dreamy. Jack thinks that you just like to argue with him."

Lina launched a couch cushion at Franca's head. "I'm not going to cave."

"I love you both," Franca said. "But you're playing marriage chicken, and I'm the one stuck watching."

The fear in Franca's voice was like heartburn. It hurt worse the harder she tried to swallow what it meant. "What do you know about being in love?" Lina sputtered.

"Less than nothing." Franca joined her on the couch and squeezed her hand. "So I guess I'm a sucky maid-of-honor."

Lina didn't notice her tears until they dribbled off her chin.

The wedding should always suit your needs and tastes, but the day belongs equally to all who come to share in the celebration. Remember, as the wedding couple, you are the star performers in an age-old pageant.

Lina bet there was a clown performing in some circus downtown wearing less makeup than she had on now.

"Oh, she's a nervous one, I can tell," the makeup artist said. "You need it for the pictures, hon. Trust me, you'll love how you look in them."

Her hair was pinned up by a crown of roses (cream, with mauve tips), and she had perfect corkscrew tendrils dangling from each ear. Lina *had* lost too much weight in her face and neck, but when she stood far enough from the mirror, she could see the illusion and not the bag of tricks. She would be beautiful in her photos, and she would be admired by all her guests. What would she be when the day was over? The answer was clear: a wife and then a mother.

Her bridesmaids seemed to jet down the aisle, and Franca,

who hadn't made eye contact all day, followed gracefully behind them. Lina took her first step, and time folded to the vows. Her shoes pinched, and she needed to scratch underneath her arm. She wasn't sure what Father Peralta was saying. She had bobby pins digging into her scalp, or maybe they were thorns. It was so hard to concentrate. She wondered if she was slowly bleeding from the head.

Jack took her hand and smiled. "I take you as my wife because my life begins and ends with you. Your love fills me up and makes me stronger. I want you as my wife because the story of our life has always been love."

Their vows were a collage of elevator love songs. Lina was about to bind her life to a man who found musak profound, yet she recited the words back to him. He was, after all, her truest friend.

Jack said, "I do," and she thought, *I don't love you*. But that was wrong. She meant *I don't gooey love you*. Even that, while not wrong, was far too simplistic.

Brides, don't be thrown off by wedding jitters. They are a natural reaction to this dramatic, life-changing event. After all, a dream wedding requires planning, but a dream marriage requires work!

Eight days after her almost-wedding, Lina's apartment had become the world's smallest labyrinth. Both her mother and Jack's had dropped off all the gifts they were storing. Neither mother was currently speaking to her, and Lina tried not to blame them. She still felt queasy, but underneath her emotional jumble, beating steadily, was relief.

Lina's wedding guide said she had a year to thank people for their presents but was strangely quiet on the etiquette of returning them. Lina had bought an Air Hitch travel voucher, so she was packing up the gifts as quickly as she could. In three-to-five days, Lina would land somewhere in Europe.

The buzzer rang three times before she could untangle herself from boxing up the Amish quilt her cousin Enza sent from Ohio. She shimmied between the two large-appliance piles, side-stepped the edge of her futon frame, and hopped over the wishing well by the door. She wasn't expecting Jack, but she should have been. He was just back from their Jamaican honeymoon. His friend Maria had taken her seat on the plane.

Lina looked at the floor, which was littered with plastic wrap and packing peanuts, then motioned him through with the scissors she held.

"You're returning them?" he said.

Lina's head jerked up. Their eyes met, and she didn't burst into flames. Being on fire might have felt better. "We can't keep them."

Jack pulled a vacuum from one of the piles. "You got cold feet." He kicked aside the paper trash, set the box down, and used it as a chair. "We're still getting married."

Lina flinched, and Jack looked away. "How was the trip?" she blurted.

After a brutal pause, he said, "You should have been there."

She sat on the edge of the box, her back to his. "I know it's lame, but I'm really, truly sorry."

"It was cold feet."

"It wasn't." Lina failed to follow up with a convincing explanation.

"Maria left her husband." He mentioned it as if they were having a casual conversation. His married friend's crush had been a long-running joke between them. Opportunist slut. Lina would track down her box and smash it. "Tell me why," he said.

Lina considered how close to the truth she could take him. "We're too different."

"Bullshit!" Jack slapped the nearest box for emphasis. "I keep you grounded."

Lina chewed her lip, resisting sarcasm.

"I hate when you get like this," he said.

Lina laughed. Indignation was the worn path in their brains. Every day together they cycled through it, so it was warm and familiar in her ears. When Jack put his thumb to the spot between her shoulder blades where she carried her tension, her body leaned into his. Her neck rolled to meet his lips, locked in the groove.

"Maria said she loves me," he breathed into her ear.

Lina jerked free. So close to relapse. "You need to leave."

He kicked the box, carving a semi-circle in the cardboard. "I hope you rot in here." He brushed past her to the stairs, which he took two at a time. "A lonely old woman with cats who feed on you to stay alive." His voice echoed in the stairwell as she shut the door.

Lina focused on breathing as she sidestepped, shimmied, and worked her way back to the half-packaged gift on the other side of the room. As she cut out squares of brown packing paper and taped and addressed one gift and then another, she thought about the possibility of being an old woman with cats, the girl who loved Cat Woman and was always in trouble, and the woman she was now, cat-free but in trouble, still.

After $\mathcal{J}$ude

$\mathcal{M}$y grandfather returned to Italy, convinced America was a soulless land that made strong men weak. My father, whose chest sank into his gut after the docks shut down and shuffled an entire neighborhood of men into the corner bar, was his proof. I can still picture them sitting silently side-by-side, dwarfing the curved, plastic seats in the airport waiting room. It was strange to see them in chairs that reminded me of my third-grade classroom, but I hadn't been to school since the trouble. That's what we called it, in the early days, before we stopped mentioning it at all.

My mother twisted her gloves in her lap, her lips moving over an urgent prayer to the Madonna as my grandfather's flight was called. My father must have made her leave her rosary behind, because she would never have forgotten it. In the neighborhood they called her St. Alma of the Black Rosary, snickering at both her piety and the cheap plastic beads she always worried. My aunts bought her a mother-of-pearl set for her birthday, but she just passed it on to me. A waste, because it languished in a box beside the bottle caps I once collected.

After Jude, I never prayed.

My grandfather picked up his suitcase, and my father said, "We all want the same thing, for her to be safe and for this to end."

"Thanks to you, it will never end," my grandfather snapped, and my father turned and walked away. He had failed in his duty to protect me, and now he was willing to break with his own father to ensure that never happened again. I wished I could believe forgetting was enough, that the nightmares would stop on their own and the memory would eventually fade away. I never chose to be their battleground.

My grandfather bent over to kiss my mother, but she turned so he could only kiss her cheek. As he placed his hand on my head, I held my breath and wished I could disappear so I wouldn't have to choose between betraying my parents or snubbing my beloved Nonno. He walked through the gate and disappeared from our lives until a telegram from the Commune di Cosenza announced his passing a year later. I was named after his home city, and now even that was tinged with death.

My mother set out on a quest for the Holy Grail of prayer, the precise invocation God required to restore the innocence I had lost. She believed the proper benediction would right all wrongs, but nothing could wipe Jude's blood from my memory. Religion had already worked against him, and I wished my aunt had named her son for anyone but the patron saint of the lost.

Jude had been a restless, questioning boy who turned bookish in his teens. Ten years my senior, I loved him because he was different from the rest of my family, and through him, I recognized my own difference without feeling entirely set apart. He spoke rarely and startled easily, unique traits among the neighborhood boys, and my uncles failed in their goal to toughen him up even when they used their fists. When he walked, his smile was always centered toward the ground, as if he had discovered some secret solace in the cracked cement beneath his feet.

After, in my dreams, he faced the sky. No act of will on my part could recreate that smile, transform the vision of his popped fish-eyes staring into the sun while the subway grate cast a checkerboard shadow across his face.

I don't know if violent movies perpetuate violence, but I can't watch them. Death has never entertained me. Every splat of blood, every snapped jaw with that awful smack sound transports me back to that afternoon when I mistook a vicious attack for boys at play.

I skipped alongside Jude, on my way home from the first of ten tap lessons I had won in our church raffle. I was thinking of how to describe my lesson in a way that would bring the most torment to my cousins when a gang of teenaged boys surrounded Jude and made him the center of their circle. Jude was shoved around, never quite allowed to regain his footing, until Benny stepped forward and the ring tightened. When I poked my head through, they closed ranks and pushed me back, leaving only peepholes between their hips. Jude and Benny argued, and I heard "I didn't" and "You did" so many times I lost count. They had been best friends once, and even then they quarreled often. Benny had carried my cousin Lina home, singing the *Sesame Street* song to distract her from the pain after she jumped off the monkey bars on a dare in kindergarten.

Jude was forced to his knees, his nose pressed to the dirty sidewalk by the pressure of his arms twisted behind his back. Then the circle broke as they all ran in different directions. Jude rolled face-first into the street, and I waited for him to pick himself up. When I finally turned him over and saw his gentle eyes protruding from their sockets, I shrieked as I should have when they first surrounded Jude. I screamed long after my father scooped me up and carried me home.

Benny, who had eyelashes so long that grown women looked at him sideways, had killed Jude with an air bubble. It worried me that two things I had believed to be harmless combined to erase Jude from my life. I began holding my breath, to wean myself in case there were other unknown mixtures to fear. I got so good sometimes I actually turned blue, but still my dreams were filled with hair dryers gone berserk and other benign items transformed into weapons.

The day the police came, my grandfather was sent to Bensonhurst to buy *scamorza*. I was told to bury my face in my mother's lap when they asked about what happened.

There were two of them, only one in uniform. Our apartment was too small for their long strides. They never sat, and their eyes absorbed everything. My mother's holy statues, the duct tape on our chairs, the mended tears in our curtains, and the roach traps covered with contact paper to make them blend into the corners.

"People in the neighborhood, they know your family? Know where you live?" The officer asked.

"My parents raised us upstairs," my mother said. "My husband grew up around the corner."

The man in the suit joined my father. He left his gold shield with me. "You should have a steel security door, or some iron bars for protection. We'll call your landlord."

My mother came out of her chair, her rosary bunched in her fist. "No trouble."

"So little work," my father mumbled, his eyes trained on the floor. "He's been fair."

The officer stood in front of our family photos. "These are your relatives in the other apartments?"

"Yes," my mother said.

"I don't think I've ever seen so many pretty girls in one family."

"You keep away from that side of the block?" The detective pointed toward the docks. "We've heard some rumors. Gang activity and the like. Just something to be aware of."

My father nodded. "We know where the bad spots are."

The officer gestured at the photos. "Nice to have family living in the building. Good company, and no one ever has to go outside alone."

The detective opened our door and looked down the stairs. "You have a spacious front hall there. Be a good place for a family dog to sleep." He stepped back inside, returned his badge to his pocket, and patted my head. "I bet the youngest ones would love a German shepherd to play with."

My mother crossed herself, a reflex against anything involving dirt and germs.

"We've got what we need," the detective said. "I don't want to have to take her to the station now. We'll save that for when we get some leads."

"If that's best," my father said, pumping his arm.

They kept looking backward as they walked down the stairs, as if they were thinking about their own families living in a place like ours.

When he found out nobody asked me any questions, my grandfather walked me to the police station himself, but the detective just drove us back home.

"I think he's confused. He keeps mentioning what happened in the war. That age, I bet."

"I'll watch him more carefully," my father said. My grandfather bought his plane ticket the very next day.

We heard Jude was killed because he stole drug money to pay for college, a rumor at least half my family believed was true. Jude had been accepted to a school in Ohio and deferred his first year to work and save money. I overheard conversations that made Jude sound snobbish and greedy, but his only crimes were finding a job when others couldn't and grabbing hold of a chance to leave, like our Uncle Paulie, yet another relative we no longer talked about.

My family wasn't the same after Jude. We weren't allowed to let our friends inside anymore, not even the ones we'd always played with, and it took a brigade of us to get permission to go even a few yards beyond our stoop. My mother kept me home from school for half a year before the truant officer came to our door.

I was thrilled to return to class, but it didn't feel the same. I listened to my classmates talk about their futures as firemen and teachers and nurses who would buy houses for their families and never, ever need food stamps again and I thought, *if they let you live that long.*

I couldn't reconnect or make new friends, and the cousins and I weren't friendly at school. It was the only time we ever had free from each other. I sank into my schoolwork, skipped a grade, and gave the valedictory speech at my elementary-school graduation.

The school called the local newspaper, and I had to smile for the camera as I was methodically embraced by strangers. I didn't need new reasons to feel divided from my peers, but once again nobody asked me.

My books were knocked from my arms the first week of junior high. "You think you're hot shit, don't you?" said a pimply, pock-marked girl I had never seen before. "Having your picture in the paper, making stupid speeches."

I had always been sandwiched between my cousins at school. Lina, the child even grown-ups feared, was stuck back in elementary and sociable, beloved Tessa was charming her way through freshman year. Both had shielded me from bullying, but this battle was mine to fight. I stared the girl down, conjuring my little cousin's ferocity and stealing her favorite line. "You may win, but I will hurt you. I'll hurt you bad."

The circle of students around us backed off, as if I could prod them with the force of my will. When she stalked off without finishing the fight she started, the other students didn't condemn her for it, or tease her unmercifully as they would have done to me. That confrontation was the first of many, because I couldn't stomach the bullying that happened every day at school. I charged whenever I spied big kids harassing little ones, but the gratitude I earned made me feel false. I was a coward who watched kin die and let killers walk free.

In high school I learned there was no statute of limitation on murder cases, and I went to the police station later that day. The detective was a sergeant now.

"Another pretty girl in the family," he said.

"I'm older now, I can testify." The words rushed out prematurely.

He stretched his arms, his eyes fixed upon mine. "You had traumatic amnesia."

"I remember now." His stare cut through me, making me feel foolish. "That happens, you know."

"You'll make big trouble for your parents. Don't make me call them."

I squeezed the vinyl armrests for courage. "I still have nightmares."

He strummed his fingers against the sole of his shoe. "No one else got hurt. I'm proud of that."

"Jude's been dead eight years."

"I saw your cousin, and so many more like him that you couldn't imagine what runs through my head at night." His attention seemed focused somewhere deep within himself, but then he pointed toward the exit. "I wish we could have saved you both, but you come from good people. They do their best in this shithole. Go home."

Was I just like him, believing other people's tragedies never compared to mine?

I left home the next year, via a scholarship to attend Jude's college. I imagined a new life that was part reunion, if not with Jude, then people I would immediately feel at home with. Reality was Nadine, my first-year roommate. She wasn't particularly pretty, but she managed to look like she belonged in a fashion magazine. I envied her polish long after she had sized me up and dismissed me. My accent seemed to be the only thing that brought her any joy. "Say *culture*! Say *on*! Say *oil*," she barked throughout the day.

When a friend admired the holes in my jeans, she said, "She didn't buy them that way."

"What difference does that make?" I challenged.

"Intent is everything," she replied. "Now say *water*."

Nadine changed my nickname, through sheer persistence, from *Enza* to *Senza*, which was Italian for *without*. Her family summered in Umbria. She knew. She saw that I was without means, but every time I heard, "Senza, hi," from even the friendliest source, it sounded like some overdue verdict.

I tried to mimic what was going on around me. I drank a lot and bed-hopped for a while, but it never felt right. I couldn't lose myself inside a keg, and sex was something that confused my brain and bored my body. I was ready to ricochet home when I overheard a round-robin of grievances in the cafeteria, the shame of having parents who bought you the wrong kind of car, were stingy with spending money, or expected you to visit on command. As I listened, I realized my family still lived hand-to-mouth while I had four fortunate years of subsidized living. I refocused on my schoolwork, as I always had before.

I was recruited by a Manhattan consulting firm straight out of college, but I had the summer free before the training program began. After four years, my family was a curtain of noise, loud and entombing. I could have rented an apartment with my signing bonus, but there were too many ways to put that money to better use. My mother dropped to her knees when I showed her the $5,000 check. When I handed her a checkbook with both our names, she shed ten years with one smile. The family bank account was in my father's name only.

I had been home a week before I spotted Benny sitting on a milk crate in the corner bodega. As I placed my skim milk on the counter, he said, "A gallon of real milk would do you fine, fill you out. But I wouldn't change nothing else."

He looked to the man behind the counter for confirmation, and the clerk said "*Guapa*," after looking me up and down.

His face was lined now, muscles blurred into flesh, but his long black lashes hadn't changed, and his light brown eyes seemed golden in the store's fluorescent light. He stared, head cocked and body loose, waiting for me to respond. I wanted to strike out at him, blunt his looks with the notches in my keys. Until I realized I could use his vanity against him.

I took my bundle from the counter and embraced it in the circle of my arms, looking him up and down as thoroughly as he had me. I sashayed past him and he followed me out, pleading to know my name as we walked down the block. I smiled, slid my hips from side to side, and said nothing.

My cousin Tessa charged off the stoop when she saw him. "What the hell you dogging her for? She don't remember!"

He looked stunned, as if recognition struck an actual physical blow. I was determined to feel nothing that would give me away. "Remember what?"

Tessa looked between us as her face flushed and grew grim. Watching her, I knew my family had grown to believe their own story, and I wished my own memory had been that malleable. "Your mother needs you," she said finally. I let her pull me up the steps, but she didn't see me turn back to wink.

I started observing the docks to get a feel for who came and went, but they were almost always deserted. Even the *bad men*, as my mother called them, had moved on. The factories, a series of closely built rectangular buildings, obscured our light and blocked our view of Manhattan. I stood on the old loading platform where my father once worked, taking in the half-standing pier, and the rot of sludge-soaked wood was enough to make me want to abandon my plan and put this life behind me.

I sat down with my feet hanging over the slimy water and looked across at the skyline. Manhattan was a world apart, its light perpetually on view yet out-of-reach. The air between appeared to have texture, like oil dripping down a sheet of glass. I was so absorbed by this that I didn't hear the cops approach me.

"It's not safe for a woman like you to be here alone," they told me the first time—every time—they met me.

"It reminds me of my grandfather. He used to fish here as a boy." The lies skipped effortlessly over my tongue.

"I bet he wouldn't like it if I told him you was here," said the larger of the two. They both looked a half-year away from playing dodge ball in the high school gym.

"He died recently," I said.

"I'm sorry about that, but it's still not safe," said the other.

"I have you to protect me," I always answered. It didn't take long to get a feel for the rhythm of the beat they walked.

Benny sat on his milk crate every day. He watched me whenever I shopped, waiting for the right moment. When I stood in the doorway, hesitating before I turned the corner opposite my own, he followed me out.

"So, what you do besides eat?" he said, putting his head inside the bag I held close.

"Not much, since I've been back. I kind of miss school, my friends, getting high."

He pulled a bag from his pocket. I shook my head. "Pot gives me a headache."

"You want some powder make you feel more alive?" he crooned into my ear.

"I prefer oblivion," I whispered into his.

He stepped back, and tilted his head as if he needed to check me out from a new perspective. "You ain't the angel you look."

I shrugged, and turned toward home. Next time he'd be prepared to entertain me.

I dressed carefully, needing to look provocative without appearing whorish. I settled on a thin silk blouse and a pleated mini that was part of a suit. My father didn't like it. "Where are you going dressed like that?"

"Into the city," was my standard answer. I tried to skirt around him, but he blocked the door.

"People are talking. They want to know why an educated girl with a fancy job is spending time on the docks."

"Maybe some people have a problem with educated girls," I said, looking more directly into his eyes than I ever thought possible. When had my father shriveled to merely my size? "Are you one of them?"

My mother only sighed and crossed herself as he barreled past us, back to his bar stool. She would continue to pray for him to stop drinking, just as she would pray for me to find peace. I preferred more direct action.

Benny showed me a leather case with a zipper as soon as I walked in. "Everything we need to float away is right in here." I lost my breath at the thought of a needle so close within his reach.

I nodded and took extra time selecting my items to calm my wheezy fears. I settled on ice cream—nobody goes off on a willing escapade with melting dairy products—and apple juice, the drink of innocents.

He suggested we go to his place, but I refused. I walked toward the docks with my groceries, and he followed. "Why doesn't Tessa like you?" I asked.

"I can't think of nothing but you now." He took my hand and pulled me through the alley between the factories and onto the brewery's old loading platform. He stood me up against the wall, and I let the bag fall from my hand. The bottle broke against the cement, and juice rolled in rivulets toward the river. He bent down, but I pressed myself against him and he abandoned his polite gesture. He leaned in, his mouth open. I could see his dental work and his tonsils.

"I like it rough," I said, and clamped down on the soft flesh of his earlobe.

He pushed me against the wall. "Damn, bitch."

I launched my tongue down his throat, and tried to divorce my mind from my actions. He grew hard against me, and I broke the kiss. "I said, I like it rough," and slapped his face. He grabbed my wrist and slammed it against the wall, squeezing my breast with his other hand as if he were milking me. "I can hardly feel that," I sneered.

He let go of my arm, and I was able to glance at my watch. I made to walk away, and the palm of his hand wedged into my mouth and forced me against the wall. I bit his hand involuntarily, as cartoon stars floated by.

He tore the buttons off my blouse, and pushed my bra down below my breasts, so they pillowed out for him. He sucked one through his teeth. I reached out to squeeze his balls, but they were just beyond my reach. He led my hand inside his zipper, and I wrapped my fingers firmly around him and squeezed, making his whole body pulse with pleasure before I dug my nails in and made him howl.

He collapsed against me, and we tumbled to the ground, where my head took another blow. He thrust himself deep inside my mouth. I couldn't breathe or even act with enough sense to clamp my teeth. His knees boxed my ears, and my head was in the puddle formed by the apple juice. I could feel bits of glass lodged into my scalp and I was sure my head was bleeding, but it felt better than any high. The more I suffered for these moments, the longer he would suffer. This time, I had fooled him.

He ripped through my pantyhose and his fingertips slipped past my underwear, but I didn't care. He eased the pressure to my mouth, and began rocking back and forth inside of me.

I clamped down with my teeth, and he howled again, backing off and lashing out, his fist connecting against my jaw, making my whole face explode with pain. I heard "Stop!" and I reached toward the voice.

I don't know if Benny realized I set him up, or being caught by the police triggered an automatic response. Either way, he bolted. They shot him, once in the leg and then twice more in the back when he kept going.

He deserved it. For the last time, if not this one. For every moment he out-breathed Jude. I'll never believe otherwise. But, for the second time in my life I was startled by death. So sudden and irreversible.

*W*eeds

*L*ina unloads two plastic containers from the trunk, then her backpack, and Eti's old military duffel while Eti hunches over the canvas sack of vegetables their former neighbors supplied, and the transporting is finally done. Now she must unpack and begin again in this, her sixth house in eighteen months, a task which grows more tiresome with each relocation: Basel, La Chaux-des-Fonds, Luzern, Lugano, Gruyère, and now Mutten. Each time, Lina leaves behind a bit of the surety that made her leave her country and cross an ocean to live with Etienne in his.

Lina's henpecked, but not by Eti. Her own doubts defeat her. Every aspect of her life here is measured against the one she left behind. She misses the certainty of her New York life, lived among friends in a language fully at her disposal. Lina's old life, however modest, was self-governed. She recognizes this value in retrospect, perhaps exaggerates it. *Perhaps. Maybe. If only. When.* Lina misses *absolutely, never in a million years,* and *right fucking now!* She rips the top off the nearest plastic tub and digs her arms in deep, as if she can find the girl she used to be inside.

Eti takes the saucepan from Lina's hand. He has her handbag slung across his shoulder. "Leave it, let's go home."

"There's too much work." He straps the purse across her shoulder. "Etienne, *s'il vous plaît.*"

Eti gets into the car and revs the engine. Some time apart

might do them good, but she doesn't want to spend the night in this strange town without him. Lina has spent most of her life seeking solitude, so this weakness is yet another estrangement from herself. She fumbles in her purse for the keys, locks the door—an *American* habit that annoys Eti—and joins him.

Eti's farmhouse, inherited from his grandparents, has become a weekend retreat while he works a job he hates, a required step to a promotion now a year past due. Lina misses the easy conversations they used to have, before they became partners in a life that is both rootless and mundane. She touches his sleeve, and he looks away from the road as if he is eager to hear her speak. She parts her lips, but her head is full of questions about the mess they left behind. She doesn't want to nag, like her burdened mother does. Her head is so heavy she slumps toward the window, and Eti stabs at the radio volume to fill the breach.

When they return late Sunday night, Eti will unfurl their futon pad and immediately fall asleep, leaving the unpacking to her. If she confronts him, he'll say that he would gladly stay home if she would go to work. Lina has tried to find a job in a café or hotel, but Americans are expected to be above such labor. No one believes she's willing to get her hands dirty, or start at the bottom in order to prove her worth. She has new sympathy for men like her father, displaced from their accustomed work. Eti earns far more than they need, but in this unequaled time of prosperity and leisure she has never felt less free.

When they arrive at the farmhouse, Lina scans the empty shelves. The shops close early Saturday and stay closed until Monday afternoon. She can't seem to plan ahead, adjust to life without twenty-four-hour access.

"I'll go see if you have any letters." Eti is out the door before she can protest. By the time he retrieves their mail from his aunt and catches up on the family news and village gossip, the shops will be closed, and she will have to borrow once again from Tante Avril's neat, well-stocked pantry.

Lina bikes into town. Neighbors nod as she passes, their faces grim as they realize that she is still in Eti's life. She tries to be friendly, but new and unusual isn't valued here, especially in a woman. The men talk to her, but only if the women aren't watching. Lina has come to view her own family, equally unfriendly to outsiders, as a tiny European village banished to the wilds of Brooklyn.

Lina's arrival disrupted the machinations of a half-dozen village mothers with unwed daughters Eti has dated or been involved with briefly over the years. Tante Avril has warned that he comes from a line of men who outgrow their restlessness. Both his father and grandfather married late and settled in the village with local wives, so the mothers will not abandon hope. When they scrutinize Lina, searching for any sign that his interest has waned in the usual way, she hates that their suspicions are so well-founded.

For a while there is nothing but green fields broken up by grazing cows, and scabs of black rock where the mountain reasserts itself. The road drops sharply at first, then gradually winds down into the valley where she crosses the wooden bridge that spans the river, swerving to avoid the fishing lines of the old men casting off the side. The chalets are close together here, aligned in brown base with white painted shutters and four symmetrical window boxes, two above and two below, filled with geraniums, always red, to set off the pristine trim.

Lina first glimpsed Eti through the hash haze of a seedy hostel in Amsterdam, barely six months after she called off her wedding. She listened, wide-eyed and eager, to stories of his two around-the-world trips, his five years as an ocean guide in New Zealand, and exotic phrases from the nine languages he had mastered. When Eti asked her to live with him in Switzerland three months later, she tore up her return ticket before she could even form an answer. She couldn't imagine spending an unhappy day in such a storied setting. Two years later she is far less naïve. There's tyranny in Switzerland's ever-manicured perfection, and the surface shine on Eti has also faded. Her worldly older man, her wild seducer, seems content to relive his adventures from the comfort of his armchair. Lina can't do this until she has some adventures of her own.

As she leans her bike against the wall of the milk store, she sees a man, obviously a stranger, trying to sell bouquets of red geraniums from a wheelbarrow to the crowd on the street. She laughs, more amused than she has been in months, because she can think of no item in all of Switzerland more ubiquitous or less valuable than a cut red geranium.

He sees her staring and extends a bouquet for her inspection. Small, dark, and too thin, he is incongruous amid strapping milk-fed blondes. It's so easy to forget that variety exists beyond this native homogeneity. She wants to tell this stranger that no one will buy his flowers. *"Parlez Français?* English?" He only proffers the bouquet each time she speaks.

She turns away, but he taps her shoulder with the stems. She looks back, and he takes one blossom from the bunch and offers it to her. She shakes him off, but his overlarge eyes implore her.

She plucks off a single petal and holds it between her fingers. It reminds her of a dream where she snipped the tops off the geraniums that line the window boxes, leaving a satisfying trail of petals. She wonders if he has acted out her fantasy. She wants to catch the Swiss in a moment of imperfection, to relish the sight of those defiled window boxes before they are quickly and efficiently replanted.

She hears a sibilant hiss coming from behind her. The catcall is a universal sound, a gesture of appreciation or simple need, understood in any language. She stops, and the stranger's voice grows sure, unintelligible phrases in a tone all-too-clear. She smiles at this sonic reminder of life back home, full of energy and complication.

A man approaches, scolds the stranger in harsh, guttural German. The stranger returns to his wheelbarrow, but as the Swiss German is about to step away, the stranger casts another glance at Lina. The Swiss German raises his hand, chokes out, "*Flüchtling.*" Refugee. Lina has also been called *Flüchtling*, but the stranger probably lives in the UN camp outside of town.

The stranger spits at the Swiss German's feet. The man sends the stranger into his wheelbarrow, which overturns. The stranger stands quickly and lunges, aiming his head at the larger man's stomach. The man deflects this charge with the flat of his palm. His hand blots out the stranger's head. The stranger rises into the air before he collapses, body twitching before it goes still. The ground is littered with geraniums. It's hard to distinguish his face from the petals.

The crowd disperses quickly, and the Swiss German man blends back into the postcard beauty of the town. A few old men right the wheelbarrow and gather up the geraniums, while the stranger lies in the street. She watches them clean up. Nobody comes to his aid or tries to help him to his feet. Is 911 an international number? Lina doesn't know, and even if she did, she can't remember which street has the town's one pay phone.

The stranger still isn't moving. She tries to stop passersby, "*Arrêtez, s'il vous plaît, cet homme exige votre aide,*" but they ignore her. The town predominantly speaks Swiss German, but she can't remember stop or help. Other German words run through her head, *danke, bitte, Flüghafen, milch, brot, wieviel,* but only *please* is useful, so she says it, *Bitte,* over and over, her voice growing louder until she covers her ears to muffle the noise she is making.

The stranger staggers away when all eyes and ears are focused upon Lina. No one will admit they saw him leave. Eti arrives and drives her back to the farmhouse. His knuckles are white against the black steering wheel. Back home, she heads straight for their bedroom, closes the shutters, and goes to bed. She doesn't sleep easily or well.

Come morning, someone raps on the front door. Eti never joined her. She feels no anger or regret, only the fear of returning home, explaining why another relationship has ended. She knows her family will blame her, out of habit if for no other reason. They dislike Etienne, even though they've only spoken to him on the phone. He's too full of himself for a foreigner. They believe Europe is a place you flee.

She considers getting up, but doesn't. A few minutes later, Eti opens the bedroom door. "Immigration is here."

She runs down the stairs, energized by the thought that they care about what happened. On a Sunday. Each of the two men who face her resembles the Swiss German man in some way. One has close-set eyes, the other unnaturally square shoulders, but she reminds herself they are here to help. Lina explains in a rush of unusually clear French. She tells them about the geranium bouquets, affects gratitude toward the Swiss German, and hopes their nurtured horror of excess will persuade them that punishment is necessary to maintain order.

When she finishes, they address Eti in rapid German, although they both speak French, and probably English, too. "They don't mind about some fight with a refugee who got out of line," Eti says. "They're here to boot you."

Her visa expired a year ago because she refused to sign a pledge to marry Eti within one year. That was a decision she'd never take lightly again. "Why now?"

"Because you got hysterical!" Eti bangs his fist into the wall, and plaster and paint chips fall from the moldings. "You shouldn't have caused such a scene."

She stamps her foot because she, too, wants to make noise. "You weren't there," she yells. "You didn't see a man lying in his own blood."

Eti cups her chin, but it doesn't soothe her. She feels like a high-strung horse he is accustomed to treating with care. "He had to learn he can't do those things here." She shakes her head from his grip. "I'm not saying it wasn't excessive, but it's not your place to criticize us."

Eti's arm slips around her waist and draws her close. He wants her to play to their audience. She slips away. "I wasn't raised on uptight neutral."

"Neutral? You accepted a flower from him—people saw you do it. Maybe that's all the permission he needs to feel entitled to you. Maybe you were saved from being dragged off."

Her mouth opens and she expects to shout, but words fail her habitually now. She moves to the closet and drags down both her suitcases. Eti escorts the two men out, his tone chatty and reassuring.

He comes back in, takes the suitcases from her and puts them back in their place. "That was good what you did. Convincing." He leads her to the couch and wraps himself around her, although she remains rigid in his arms. "I told them I'm driving you to France tonight, that I was tired of all the fighting."

He nuzzles against her ear, and his breath is so warm that it is hard not to melt into him, blot out the space between. Their bodies hold no grudges. "Stop it," she says, as her toes begin to curl.

"It was a mistake to spend so much time here. You need to settle in somewhere without so many eyes upon you." He knows her well, despite their differences. "We'll go to Mutten, forget about this place for a while?" he croons.

His hands are everywhere, like a tree sprouting new branches. "We're not getting along."

"Bah—that's the American in you talking. We have the rest of our lives to work that out." He runs his fingertip across her forehead, down the bridge of her nose. "I don't want to lose you," he whispers. "Tell me you won't leave."

His voice is a command, and she nods.

"I'll talk to Tante Avril. She'll help us. Tell everyone you've gone back to America." Eti pulls her along with him, and they part with a long, slow kiss by the door. She watches him walk down the road, aware of all the places where he touched her. She spins around, resisting the urge to catch up and continue what he started in the grass, until she spots a glint of orange at her feet.

Her marigolds, in the ground. Arranged in neat, evenly-spaced rows.

She looks up at her window boxes, and they are filled with red geraniums. She supposes she should be grateful her flowers were transplanted, since Tante Avril told her marigolds are merely weeds. The soil's not freshly tilled, but it's hard to believe her eyes skipped over them when she arrived. Her fists spasm as Eti's heat leaves her body. She rips the geraniums out by their roots and goes inside to pack.

Seventeen

"Do you think the Protestants could be right? About the Holy Trinity being separate and all?" Bo asked.

Kate pulled the blanket from his legs and covered the wet spot, which he always managed to avoid comfortably. He left her with the bed's edge, the end table poking her shoulder. She didn't understand why men had to spread their legs so wide. They did it on the subway benches, sponging up whole seats, and Bo was doing the same thing here. She didn't care how much bigger he was, how he made the full-sized mattress seem so small. She hated how it never occurred to him to take up less than his share. That she had to, by default, she hated even more.

"You never answer me when I ask you things," Bo complained.

"I don't understand why you need to talk religion after." Kate poked his shoulder, but he moved closer, annexing more territory. "It makes me think of sin, of dead relatives watching everything I do."

"We're not sinning." Bo laid his arm across her stomach. "I'm going to marry you, when you're old enough."

Kate loved the curve of his forearm, his protruding vein a well-marked trail to the sudden drop at his wrist. Bo had been her adolescent wakeup, her unrequited urge, her first kiss. "You're supposed to ask, you know."

"We could fly to Vegas with my signing bonus and get married by Elvis on your birthday."

"Elvis is dead, Bo." Needing space, Kate used him. He was firmer than the mattress, a wedding gift that outlasted her parents' marriage. How long could marriage with Bo last? He dropped out of community college after football season. Almost two years in remedial and he still couldn't pass the exams he needed to transfer, but he'd go in the next draft as a defensive tackle. Not early like he would have with a couple of years playing on a Big East team, but he'd go. That was enough to get him out of the neighborhood, and Kate with him.

Kate's grades weren't that great, but her SAT scores were in the 95th percentile. Her high school guidance counselor still suggested vocational school. Rae, her mom, bounced between their apartment and a psychiatric halfway-house, so Kate's dreams had to be practical. Night college after she found a steady secretarial job. Katharine Gibbs had already cashed her tuition deposit. She never told Bo about the money. He expected his wife to travel with the team.

Bo flipped her onto her back, but her thoughts stayed with her two possible futures until his presence became a distraction. He was anvil shaped, broadest in the chest and shoulders. Bo was designed for the action-oriented close up, that breath-catching moment of absolute desire. Unfortunately, the beginning of her pleasure time always signaled the tail end of his.

Kate reached down for her ankh-shaped hairpin, which had fallen. She had found it at the club where she waitressed, and she liked the engravings of interlocking swirls. She didn't want Bo crushing it when he ran for the bathroom, like her glasses last week. Kate stretched out her arm a bit further, twisting just as Bo collapsed on her. She heard the snap before she felt the pain in her side. The time lapse made her think whatever had cracked couldn't possibly belong to her.

"Oh shit," he said, rolling off. The motion made her inhale wrong, and she started coughing. Firecrackers went off inside her chest, exploded in batches down her left side. "I think that bulge is one of your ribs."

"You broke my rib?" she screamed. "You asshole!" Screaming was bad.

"Don't get hysterical." Bo sat with his pants in his lap, dusting off carpet fuzz. "I've played with a couple of cracked ribs."

"Fucking Christ! I'm not on the god-damned team."

He said, "Don't blaspheme at me." She stood up, opened her mouth to blaspheme some more, and passed out. When she came to, she was wearing sweatpants and he was trying to get her bra fastened. He pointed at the floor and said, "Those jeans are way too tight."

She thought, *You never mind when you're looking at my ass,* but remained quiet. She was too scared to fight.

Bo picked her up carefully, but she started coughing again. In the car, he said, "If we don't tell them the truth, they're going to think maybe I hit you. If they call the cops and it gets in the papers, it's over for me. No draft. Bad boy. Bad risk."

"What if the truth gets in the papers?"

Bo didn't answer during the drive. Later, after she'd been grinned at, whispered over, poked, x-rayed, doped, and taped up while he was surreptitiously pointed out and admired, he said, "Maybe now they'll draft me earlier."

�֍

Kate waitressed Thursdays and Fridays at a club called Santé, in the old meatpacking district just beyond the West Village. It maintained its popularity by changing themes every six weeks, and the new one was "endangered species." There was faux fur everywhere and musk was pumped through the air ducts. The heavy scent made it even harder to breathe. Her new uniform was an animal-print bikini-top and a black lycra miniskirt. Her taped-up midriff wasn't the look they were going for. "Go home," Tracey, the club manager, told her.

"Will you pay me?" she asked.

"What do you think?"

"I think Workman's Comp might have a few questions about having a seventeen-year-old on your payroll for a year."

"What makes you think you're on the payroll?" he spat out.

"Tracey, please." He was from her neighborhood, had taken Kate's mother to her high school prom, but he'd never let her ruin this gig for him. He told people he was from the Upper West Side, the rebel child of two Columbia professors, and they believed him. He didn't even sound like he came from Brooklyn.

"Can you even lift a tray?" Kate pulled one off the bar. She clipped her tongue, tasted blood. She had Tylenol with codeine for the pain, but it wasn't working right. "You have a black leotard in your locker?"

"I've got a couple in there," she said.

"Just wear the top over the leotard, then, and don't forget this the next time I need you to cover a shift," Tracey said.

"I always take the extra shifts anyway." Kate didn't want to be grateful.

She usually spent her break reading in a closet behind the VIP room, but she needed to lie on her back for a while, to stop the constant jabs. She went to the peace pit, a section of the converted burlesque theatre that had small, private performance spaces. The club had taken out the chairs and carpeted the stacked floor, creating plush bleachers for "relaxation." This wasn't the singles section; as she made room for herself in the middle row, she tried to ignore the invitations. Finally, she just put her book over her face and pretended not to hear.

Someone tilted the book off her cheek and put it down again. "I find you in the strangest places, Kate."

Cameron was a regular. Went to Yale, although he was at the club most nights. Kate wanted to ask him what it was like, but she never would. He left her books as tips. *Ironically.* She read them anyway.

"Heard your boyfriend mistook you for one of his soccer balls."

"Football," Kate said. "Bo plays football, and he could break you in two with one hand."

"Been practicing that trick, has he?"

"It was an accident." Kate tried to sit up, but tortoise-like was still too fast.

"Now, however are you going to rise above your trailer-trash existence if you resort to that tired old line?" He pulled a tobacco pouch from his pocket and rolled a cigarette. "You're not going to say, 'But Cameron, I love him' next, are you?"

"I don't live in a trailer."

"Minor technicality." He took a long drag, held his finger up as if testing the air, took a few steps away from her and exhaled, waving the smoke away before he came back. "A city built out of islands has finite space and trailer parks don't stack well. If you lived anywhere else in this great nation, it would be the trailer for you, babe."

"I despise you," she said.

"You despised me before you ever knew me, you snob." He picked up *Jude the Obscure,* which he left for her a few weeks back. "Page 286, huh? I couldn't get past the first fifty. You must be smarter than you look."

Kate stood up slowly, her spine taking a long time to straighten. "I'm only working here for the intellectual reward."

"Whatever. No one takes Hardy seriously anymore." He walked away and came back with someone's purse in his hands. "Try these." He handed her a bottle of pills. "Two should get you through your shift."

"You're a doctor now?" she asked.

"Just shut up and take them." She didn't see him again that night, but the pills worked. He left a $100 tip on the table, stuffed between the pages of *Grendel.* She was tempted to take the book and leave the cash behind.

❂

At the supermarket where she worked after school she was taken off the cash register and assigned throwbacks, returning the items customers left behind. The other cashiers were miffed; she was hogging up the only chore that gave them a breather from the endless lines of customers. It wasn't even helping. Pushing the cart made her rib buckle and stab, especially when the wheels caught and reversed from all the scuff marks on the floor. Bending up and down was even worse. She asked for a week off, but they refused. She ran out of the pills Cameron gave her three days ago, and she hadn't been to school since. It was too hard to get out of bed in the morning. Besides, she already knew how to alphabetize, add, subtract, and format a business letter.

Bo tore through the double doors of the produce room with a smack. His brother-in-law was the produce manager, and Bo slacked his way through the off-season in the back room. He took the cart from Kate and started throwing stuff randomly on the shelves. "Stop it!" she said, picking up after him. "I'll get in trouble."

"They won't fire you," he said, sending a Spam container for a touchdown. It broke apart at the other end of the aisle, a few feet from an unattended child who started screeching. Bo shrugged, said, "They know you're my girl."

"Why don't you get me a week off, then?" She walked over to the meat counter and asked them to call maintenance to clean up the spill. She motioned for Bo to push the cart over to the next aisle.

"You don't look good," he said, when he joined her.

"I feel like crap." She fought back tears. She would not cry in the middle of the frozen food aisle.

"It's been almost a month. It's supposed to get better."

"Look, I'm not you. I can't forget that it hurts and still win the game." She put a half-melted can of orange concentrate back, sticking it behind the others so it would have a chance to freeze. She took one of the frozen cans and put it to her head. The ice felt good against her forehead.

"I think maybe you should call your mother and tell her to come home for a while," Bo said. From the crease settling in at the wide bridge of his nose, she knew he was concerned about her.

The fear that something might actually be wrong made him want to pass on responsibility to someone else.

"She's not exactly at a hotel, you know." Kate pointed at the case of Budweiser in the cart. He looked confused. "Lift it for me, please."

He picked up the case, slung it back on the shelf like he was flipping the ball. She left it and motioned him forward. "What makes you think having my mother back would make things better?"

"She's pretty cool sometimes." Bo helped himself to an economy-size bag of Doritos, leaving a trail of crumbs as he steered the cart with one hand and ate with the other. "She lets us drink at your place, doesn't mind if I come over, she doesn't hassle you about curfews and stuff. My parents are total stiffs."

"How silly that they fed and clothed you and bought you a car for graduation, when all you really wanted was for them to crack open a beer with you every once in a while."

He listened to a request for a price check in produce over the intercom. "I don't know why you're defending them. My mother can't stand you."

"I know," she said. She expected it to sound defiant. She cupped her hand over her rib and held her breath. If she applied pressure to the right spot and didn't breathe, the pain eased momentarily.

"Call your grandmother," he said.

"I call my grandmother every day."

"Yeah, but you don't ever tell her nothing." He was paged by name on the intercom this time, but he only looked toward produce. "Maybe Father Peralta could help."

"How?"

"A special prayer or a blessing." Bo's voice jumped an octave. He hated it when she scoffed at his religious convictions. They were supposed to be hers, too.

"Will you drive me to the club after your shift ends?" she said, as he was paged again.

"Why do you want to go there?"

She hesitated but couldn't come up with a convincing lie. "Those pills really helped."

"You don't even know what they are." He swerved the cart around to face her. "No way."

Kate took the cart from Bo and said, "I'll just take the subway, like I always do."

※

"I didn't see you last night," Kate told Cameron when he sat at one of her tables.

"You don't work Wednesdays," he said.

"I was looking for you," she said. "I thought you lived here."

"The pops was in town. Had to have dinner at 21 so he could feel parental." He took the pad out of her apron and wrote down his drink order, then placed it back in the pocket and aligned the ends of her apron strings. Cameron had an eye for imperfection. "If I'd known you were finally going to give me the time of day, I'd have blown him off."

She stepped out of reach. "Cut it out."

"You're so prickly, Kate." He lunged for a drink on a passing tray, and she had to swat his hand away. The sudden movement made her gasp. "You make it so hard for a man to court you."

"Court me?" she asked, just to be sure she heard it right. "You don't want to court me, you want to fuck me. I know the difference."

"Actually, I just want to fuck with you. That's a whole class of different."

"Great," she said. "I'll get your drink now."

"That rib still giving you trouble?" he shouted, when she was halfway to the bar. He timed it perfectly to a pause in the vocals. Half her customers turned her way. She kept going.

"What do you care?" she asked, when she brought his vodka martini. She had the bartender pour it in a margarita glass to gall him.

Cameron held the glass up to his eye and looked through it. "How many pills you have left?"

"What were they?" she asked. "Legal?"

"When prescribed." He pulled out his tobacco pouch, felt around for his lighter. "You need more?"

She nodded, her eyes trained on her tray.

"I'll see what I can do."

He had a full bottle for her within an hour, and she took three. Now she was pain free, although she still felt the strain of clean breaths. It just didn't seem to matter. It was hard to count out change, but her bad mood lifted. Then Bo showed up to drive her home. Her shift wasn't over for three more hours. She took him into the back room and said, "It's the busiest time of night, I can't baby-sit you."

"You look good," Bo said, looking behind her into the main bar. She looked where he did, but the lights from the dance floor beyond bounced into her eyes. You could never look higher than eye level here without being blinded by the strobes. She turned away from the doorway. "Where's your friend?"

"What friend?" she asked.

"The drug lord."

"I'm more like a pharmacist who takes requests," Cameron said, over her shoulder. He had his chest puffed out and his arms behind his back.

"Cameron, you know you can't be back here."

Cameron cocked his head in Bo's direction. "He's back here."

"Tracey hates it when you act like you own the place," she said.

He pulled his glass from behind his back. "I need a refill."

Kate waved her arms at him, forcing his retreat. "Okay, okay. Go sit down."

"You're not going to introduce me to your boyfriend?" he asked, as he backed out of the room.

Kate pointed a finger at one, then the other. "Cameron, Bo."

Bo held out his hand. "Tony Bonanno."

Cameron handed Kate the empty glass, clicked his heels, and bowed slightly. "Cameron Alexander White, III."

Kate left before they started pissing on the barstools. When she brought Cameron's martini to his table, Bo was sitting with him. "Bring my buddy a beer," Cameron said. "You're a beer man, right?"

Bo shook his head. "Already had a few tonight, and I gotta drive my girl home soon."

Cameron nodded, slid his drink away from Bo as if it might contaminate his purity. "Precious cargo."

"Damn right." Bo slapped the edge of the table, sending a shockwave that knocked the glass on its side.

Kate picked up the glass, put the napkins she had over the spill. "I'll go get a rag." When she came back, they were slapping each other on the back. Kate wiped down the table and stood there.

"So tell me, what do you two lovebirds do together?" Cameron asked.

"What do you mean?" Bo said, his face beginning to flush. Kate figured he thought it was a sex question.

"I mean what I asked. You're in love, you spend a lot of time together. What do you do? What do you talk about?"

"We do what normal couples do. We hang out. We talk a lot."

Cameron sat back and cupped his chin. "Anything special you do together?" It was his shrink pose. Kate had seen him use it on depressed NYU girls.

Bo squirmed in his seat. He only knew how to be admired. "What are you after? We're not like that. We go to church on Sundays."

"Church? Church!" Cameron gleefully abandoned his pose. "Now, Kate, I wouldn't have pegged you as religious."

Kate wanted to say, "I never go to church," but she hugged her tray instead.

"She's a good Catholic," Bo said. Cameron rolled a cigarette, giving the process his full attention. Bo put both hands flat on the table, and suddenly it looked small, like a child's play toy. "You think because she reads those books you give her, that you know her? You don't know Katie."

Cameron lit his cigarette and took a long drag. He held his breath for effect, and then let the smoke out slowly through the straight, neat bands of his teeth. "You're right, I definitely don't know K-k-katie at all."

Bo knocked the table over with a flick of his wrist. Kate shoved all her weight against him, trying to move him toward the door. Her rib screamed like it had its own lungs. Bo moved in millimeters. "You can't do this, I'll get fired. Go and come back at five." She slapped at his chest. "I mean it. Go."

"If I leave, I'm going home."

"Fine. I can get myself home." Tracey was making his way through the crowd on the dance floor. "Get out of here." Bo bent to kiss her, but she jerked her head away. Tracey nodded at her as Bo headed for the exit.

Cameron righted the table, held his hand out to Tracey, who didn't shake it. "It was my fault, I was just having a bit of fun with him. Don't get on her for this."

"I'll get your drink," she said, leaving. Tracey followed on her heels.

"I don't care if Captain America kicks the living shit out of that little prick," he said. "Just keep it out of my club."

Kate swallowed hard, her mouth dry, and nodded. "Give him his drink on the house," Tracey said, and elbowed his way back through the dance crowd.

Kate handled her other customers before she brought him his drink. Cameron didn't touch it, just stared at her until she said, "What?"

"I know you're a pragmatist, Kate, but I hope you realize you can aim higher than that." Kate slid his drink closer, and turned to the couple that sat down a few tables over. "That was a compliment," he shouted over the music.

"Excuse me a moment," she said to the couple, edged back to Cameron. "You're the expert?"

"I was just saying—"

"What have you ever had to aim for?" If not for Tracey, she'd have flipped the table over herself. She checked on all her other customers. When she passed by next, he was gone. He left her *The House of Mirth.*

She walked across the bar to his friends, the ones that wouldn't sit in her section any more, and aimed the book at their table. The spine hit the edge and bounced before falling under a chair. She enjoyed watching them flinch and jerk away. No one bothered to retrieve it, but that didn't matter. They'd let him know.

※

Kate was having trouble counting out her register. Three times she counted, three times she had wildly different totals. It was brag day at school, and she had to sit through a three-hour assembly where they announced the college tallies for the senior class. All the top students got to talk about their choices. Ninety-three percent of her class was going on to college. Kate rode the subway an hour each way to get to this school because they had such a good reputation, because at the local high school the college entrance rate was probably reversed. An extra ten hours a week for three years, and she still wasn't any better off. Maybe at the other school she would have stood out more, maybe someone would have tried to help her get a scholarship somewhere. It never occurred to her that her extra effort would amount to nothing. For this alone she felt like a fool.

On her way home, she saw her neighbor's boy on the long, wide steps of Saint Anthony's. He was trying to play jacks, but the ball and jacks he had were too large for his hands. He couldn't catch the ball without the jack leaking from his grip. "My mom said to look out for you."

"What's wrong?" She caught the ball for him as it ricocheted off the heel of his palm.

"Your mom's back."

Kate flung the ball against the ground, and the bounce it took reached almost as high as the cross hanging from the roof. The ball bounced four more times before he could catch it. "Wow, do that again, Kate."

"Thank your mom for me, okay?" She left him bouncing the ball in the air, trying to match her distance.

Kate heard Patsy Cline lamenting love from halfway down the street. Three flights up, the two front windows were wide open. Her mom's stereo was in her bedroom in the back. The women sitting on the stoop stared at the gum-pocked steps as she squeezed by. Mrs. Kozinski placed a scapula in her hand, blessed by the pope from her native Krakow. Kate had a dozen others stuffed in a drawer. "Katie, just go to grandma's. It's better for you, hon."

Kate nodded slightly and kept going. Both her grandfather and her Great-Aunt Alma were sick, with prostate cancer and glaucoma. Her grandmother had enough burdens.

At the door, all the locks were set, including the chain and the floor bolt. "Mom, it's Kate. You have to let me in. Rae." She yelled over the music, trying to stretch out the chain so she could squeeze enough of her head through to look for her mother. She had to wait for the lull between songs to get her attention.

Her mother took a long time opening the locks. She kept changing her mind about the order, accidentally relocking instead of unlocking, while crooning, "Mama's coming, Katie-baby, just a minute, babygirl, hold on, Katie-pie, Mama's here now."

When her mother finally got the door open, she launched herself into Kate's arms, setting off shivers that reached her fingernails. Kate stood for a moment, absorbing the pain before she kissed her mother's cheek. She went to the bedroom to turn down the music. Her mother held on, dragging behind her. "I heard Patsy down the block," she said. "Do you want the police to come again?"

Her mother detached herself and fell to the bed with a sigh. "Sgt. Joe said he'd take all my records next time."

Kate joined her mother on the bed, spreading out next to her. Her body just wanted to stay there forever, weave itself into the worn threads of the sheets. Her rib was starting to give off a kind of heat that meant the pain was about to double. This was when her head got fuzzy, and it was hard to make her eyes stay focused. "Let me see," her mother said.

Kate lifted up her shirt, showed her the tape across her middle. They had retaped her last week, after her six week check-up. She wasn't healing. "Did Bo call you?"

"He said you fell down and hurt yourself." Her mother ran her fingers along the edges of the tape, wrapped a stray strand around her finger and was about to pull but stopped. She unwound the strand and smoothed it back along the edge of the tape line, then very deliberately put her hands flat against her own ribcage. That tiny bit of restraint was an encouraging sign. "Why didn't you tell me?"

Her mother's voice, naturally loud, seemed to come from outside the room, like the tinny sound of a bad phone connection. Was this how the world sounded to her mother? So remote it was barely worth answering? Was going through this a way to finally understand her?

"Katie girl? Are you listening?"

"I didn't want to worry you," Kate said automatically. She pulled two pills from her bag and stood up slowly. She needed water. In the kitchen, the fridge was open, and the cabinets were empty. All the food was stacked on the table.

"I was going to cook for you," her mother said.

The glasses were lined up in a row along the counter by the sink. Kate took one from the middle, filled it with water. On the other side of the sink, there were rows of cups and soup bowls. The plates were stacked on the window sill. Kate swallowed the pills and emptied the glass of water. "You can't stay."

"I am staying," she said. "I'm the mother. You need me."

"Don't go there—I don't want to fight. You know you can't take care of me, and I can't take care of you right now. I'm sorry, but I just can't." Kate picked up the stack of plates and put them back in the cabinet.

"I'm organizing all that," her mother said. "I'm here to take care of you."

Kate brushed past her and pointed at the fridge. "Why is this door open? Why did you have to take out all the food?"

"I had to see what we had." She leaned forward with her hands at her hips, and looked like a chicken about to peck. "How else do you plan a meal?"

"Who's going to put all this stuff away? You have to go back."

"No."

"Where are your pills?" Kate asked.

"I'll take my medicine. Every pill, I swear. I will."

"Show me."

"I'll get some. Tomorrow. First thing."

"Genovese is still open," Kate said.

"No, tomorrow. I promise."

Kate reached for the phone. She had the number on speed dial. "Hi. Who is this? Jackie? Hi, it's Kate Connelly. I need the van to come pick up my mother... I know she checked herself out."

Her mother started marching around in a circle, calling out, "Tomorrow, tomorrow, tomorrow," in progressively louder tones.

Kate held out the phone so Jackie could hear. "She'll be out-of-control soon," she said, then, "No, I won't leave her, but I need to be at work by ten."

⊛

Santé closed at four, and by the time she cleaned up it was five-thirty. She never took the subway home before seven, so she waited at the all-night diner down the block. It was the old trailer variety, and it was a popular spot for breakfast with the Santé crowd. Nico the night manager made his special Armenian stuffed grape leaves on Fridays. He always saved a plate for Kate, but tonight she couldn't eat. She showed up at the club late, then spent half the night sobbing in the back room. Even Tracey didn't have the heart to chew her out. He loved Rae once, too.

The door chimed and Cameron walked through. Nico came out from behind the counter with his bat in his hand. A few months back, Cameron and his friends were roughed up by some guys from Bensonhurst, who wrecked the place in the process. Nico hadn't let him in since. For a golden boy, Cameron had real trouble making friends.

Cameron threw his arms up, pointed his finger in Kate's direction. "I just want to see if she's okay. I can drive her home if she's not feeling well." Nico took a practice swing. Kate felt the swish. "Just let me ask her." He leaned in Kate's direction, his arms protecting his head. "Will you call him off me, please?"

"I'm off duty," she said. Nico charged and Cameron pleaded.

"Let him stay if he wants," she said finally.

He slid into her booth and stared at her. She ignored him. "Some women can get away with the splotchy skin and the red-rimmed eyes. You are not one of those women."

Kate's indifference wilted. "Did you come here to insult me?"

"It's not an insult," he said. "I've never wanted to kiss you more."

"Leave me alone."

"My parents, me, I don't think we feel anything for each other—fuck, that's trite." Cameron gestured to Nico. "Maybe he should come club me with that bat."

Kate covered her ears. "Don't play the all-families-are-crazy game with me. It's humiliating."

"Last year, on my birthday, I found out my mother can't remember my middle name. I think the bare-bones requirement for motherhood should be that you remember what you wrote on the birth certificate."

Kate smiled briefly. They both sat quietly for a while.

"What about your father?" he asked.

Kate never thought about her father much. Her mother took up too much time. "He was nice, but he died when I was ten."

Cameron nodded. "I think my father is the most selfish prick I've ever met."

"Considering the crowd you run with, that's pretty frightening."

"I know." Again he seemed sincere. "I can drive you home, if you want."

Kate shrugged. "I don't want to go home."

"Then tell me what you want."

Kate snorted. In Cameron's world, naming a desire was the only obstacle. "I want to not be me. Just for a little while. Can you make that happen?"

"I know a way," he said. "But I'm not sure you'd go for it."

"What?" There were no rules tonight.

"Smack," he said, as if it was obviously the only choice.

Kate tried to imagine his tailored friends slapping their veins, cooking brown liquid on a spoon over a candle flame. She couldn't, not the how or the why. "How very retro. Here I thought you couldn't wait to get me all coked up and in bed."

"Coke doesn't make you want to leave the world, it makes you want to rule the world. Besides, sex is better on heroin."

Kate lifted her brows. "Why?"

"Imagine an orgasm that's less centered, less intense, but lasts as long as the high—or as long as you can stay focused on sex— you tend to drift in and out of things." Kate looked away, drank the last of her coffee. Cameron leaned over the table. "Is Bo the only guy you—"

Kate nodded incrementally. He said, "You've never—"

"None of your business."

"Come on." Cameron slapped a fifty on the table. "This much I promise I can do for you."

In the car, on the way to his apartment on the Upper East Side, he rested his hand in her lap. Kate thought to push him off, but his hand was still and she felt warm and aware. His fingers began to nudge softly, a timid arc that seemed harmless until her legs drifted apart and his hand glided smoothly under her skirt, past the thin strip of underwear. He rested the heel of his hand there. She waited for his move, but he made no move. She had to force herself to be still as the car stopped and started. She watched him drive. He was focused on the road, seemingly unaware of her while she fixated on what he was— wasn't—doing to her. Her teeth were grinding, made tense by the building warmth that seemed entirely her own doing. He was merely driving.

He curled a finger, then another, inside her. She leaned into them, her body relaxing into the seat, then lurched as his thumb started working her tip. When he turned into an underground lot, she didn't want the ride to be over, felt the hard disappoint- ment of being cut short. Again. She expected him to pull his hand free and get out of the car, but he braked into a spot and shifted the gear with his left hand. He leaned across her, his shoulder digging into her chest, and shifted her seat back. He shook his free hand at her and said, "Elbow room," with a wicked smile.

They kissed for the first time. He climbed over the gear shift to get on top of her, get his arms more fully around her, deepen the kiss, stretch out the places where they touched. The pain was somewhere in the background, shoved aside by the prospect of pleasure. She was dazzled by her body's fireworks, confused by the order of things, by how much she wanted him. "You live alone?" she asked, when they breathed. She swallowed another pill as she waited for his answer.

"Right upstairs. Elevator. Fourteen floors."

She had his jacket off before the elevator doors shut, and she let it drop to the floor. He lifted her, leaned her back against the wall, held her tighter as he grew still. Once again, she seemed to be the restless, impatient one. "What's wrong?" she asked, as he lowered her to her feet.

"Conscience." He had to squeeze the word out. "You're not yourself."

The doors opened and she walked off as he froze. She waved her arm at the sensor to keep the door from shutting. "Don't you dare ruin this."

The hallway was large, with hotel-like décor. There was tan

carpeting, two armchairs, and lines of doors on both the left and right. It was much more institutional than she expected. "You'll hate me tomorrow," he said.

She laughed, a sharp bark that exploded from her, made her rib echo. As if sex could change the nature of their relationship.

❉

When she woke up, there was pain. Her pills were in her bag, but her bag was still in his car. Cameron wasn't in bed with her. She listened for sounds of him, but the apartment was quiet. It was large, but it was also spare. She expected something grander, something from a magazine. He had his own bar, and he was only two years older than she was. He had skipped a few grades. Said he was making up for them now.

It was after four, and her supermarket shift had already started. Her rib hurt so bad she couldn't move. For once, she didn't try. He could get the pills for her when he returned. Soon, she hoped. She should have realized last night that her rib would be balky this morning, but morning hadn't mattered last night.

It wasn't only her rib, either. She was sore all over. If she could get herself to move, she'd take a hot shower or soak in his bathtub, which was the size of an inflatable kiddie-pool. He said it had jets, but they never made it into the tub like they planned. Sex had never seemed so…urgent. Cameron didn't weigh much more than she did, and it was as light between them as sex with Bo had grown heavy. They wrestled, evenly matched, and they laughed. He was interested in her body, and he asked her questions she couldn't answer. Gradually she found the words. He read to her, poems at first—a dirty one about a car that was really a woman—and then from any book she pulled from the shelves that lined his bedroom, every room, in his apartment.

His eyes were a blue-green that morphed with the light. She never noticed that in the dim lights of the club. She had thought of them as bored, contemptuous, demanding, but never lovely, like the line of his jaw and his prominent collarbone. When she rested her head against his chest, he was bony but not oppressive. She fell asleep tangled with him and didn't feel hemmed in.

Cameron obliterated any illusions she had of a future with Bo. She wasn't sure if she liked him very much, but that felt irrelevant. He had recognized something in her, something she considered special about herself that no one else ever seemed to see. Even so, she feared the day when all his worldly contempt turned on her. For real. It seemed too much a part of him to ever be sidestepped. What if that was happening now? What if Cameron wasn't coming back? Maybe some stranger, someone Cameron paid, would come offer her a speedy shower and cab fare home. Maybe everything that happened between them was planned with this result dense and heavy in his mind. Maybe all he recognized was just how easy she would be. All he had needed was patience. As time clicked by in stabs, this reasoning became absolute, and satisfaction passed into remorse.

When Cameron returned, she was turning blue. Her eyes were bloodshot, and her breaths were shallow gasps. Both hands were pressed against her side, as if they were all that held her rib inside. He dialed 911 but put the phone back in its cradle before the operator came on the line.

"You're just hyperventilating, Kate. You need to calm down and breathe right."

She could hear him but was beyond understanding.

"Relax! Please! That's all you need!" He jumped around her, then sat on the bed and emptied the bag he brought with him onto the bed. He wrapped the tubing around her arm and this time, he served her. Kate would appreciate the irony later. He bit on his tongue as he pricked her arm, a vein at the base of her wrist. Her hand fell to her side before the plunger was all the way down. The tightness washed from her face and her color returned as her breathing normalized. The nausea followed next, and he helped her to the bathroom.

Her stomach was empty, leaving only dry heaves that made her body tremble. Her rib didn't worry her. Nothing worried her. She was astral. A star floating in the crowded sky. A speck in the universe. How hard could the life of a mere speck be? She embraced her speckiness. Found this revelation insignificant. Moved on.

She sat on the floor, her back against the side of the bed. She had a portion of his Oriental rug in her lap, and she grasped at its edges as she stared at the pattern. Order existed within this rug. It was communicating with her, about to reveal something only she had the brains to look for. She nodded off, into blankness. A fold in the universe grabbed her and let her go, grabbed her again. And again. Like a man. Pain couldn't reach her. She was an embryo again, unformed, or maybe the arms of God were around her. If so, religion finally made sense.

She wasn't sure if she slept. Her eyes were open, but it took a while to see. To remember about seeing. She was back in bed, shifted on her good side. Her mouth was dry. Cameron was running his finger across her forehead, and she wanted him to scratch. "Time?" she asked.

"Eleven-thirty," he said, added "P.M." when she looked scared.

"I should go home. I have to work tomorrow." As she said this, she knew she wouldn't. The bed was plush and warm, and she had room.

"Stay the night," he said. "I'll drive you tomorrow. You won't miss it." He still had his hand on her forehead.

"What are you doing?"

"You're too young to have lines. I'm smoothing them out for you."

"Did we have sex?"

"You don't remember?" His face turned rosy. She didn't think he knew how to blush.

"I mean just now. It's fuzzy, but you said..."

"You didn't even know I was in the room." He tried brushing the hair from her face, but his fingers caught in the tangles. "It was business as usual."

She felt weird. Limp, but relaxed. Her heart was beating really fast, but nothing felt wrong, exactly. "I need a bath. And food. Food would be excellent."

"Eating should wait, or you'll get sick."

"How was it for you?"

"I can't shoot myself—too squeamish."

"You didn't get high?" she asked.

"I just watched you." She thought about him watching her and was prepared to be disturbed. But the feeling just didn't take.

"I feel better," she said. "I needed every minute of this."

He snorted, rolled onto his back. "Glad to be of use."

"What, you don't like that feeling?"

"Stay the night," he commanded.

"Only if I get a bath, some food, and some sleep."

"You're awfully demanding." He chewed at a fingernail, as if deciding. "Do you tip well?"

"That depends upon the service," she said. "I might have a book or two I can spare."

He took the portable phone from its recharger and went into the bathroom to run the water for her. "Do you like Indian food?"

"I've never had it," she said.

He poked his head back into the room. "Pizza?"

"No," she said, slowly sitting up against the headboard. "I want to try."

He ordered for them both and then helped her into the tub, where the jets pulsed hot water scented with eucalyptus oil around and against her. "I use that stuff for hangovers," Cameron said.

She closed her eyes and tried to breathe deeply. Tomorrow she would go home and face her life. Tonight she would take what Cameron offered. Tonight she liked him, and tomorrow was hours away.

Bouquet

*Y*ou don't expect to find beauty amid blight, never plan to visit a place you think of only in terms presented by the media—hatred, war, atrocity. You finance your trip with an unexpected winning streak at the roulette wheel in Monte Carlo. Although you have the money you need for a ticket home, you travel east instead, to see the remnants of a world that passed into history. You are not the only American peeking behind the Iron Curtain. You meet your third-grade teacher on a tour for retired nuns in Krakow, dine on pork-fried fruit in Budapest with a half-starved vegetarian, and flee Prague when a woman from your native city staggers up to you, slurs, *They put something in the beer here, man,* and vomits on the only dress you aren't sick of wearing.

You shift back west but change your mind in sleepy Ljubljana, where you hitch a ride to Sarajevo on a humanitarian-aid truck. You aren't a convert to good deeds, just bored with the all-day train ride to a place you've already been. A coffee-stop conversation with the British driver is all it takes to change your mind.

Sarajevo links to a round-cheeked boy with cartoon eyelashes who rewarded you for stopping a soccer ball with your face during gym class in junior high. You saved the game and his pride, and he gave you a finger puppet of Vucko, the mascot from the Sarajevo Olympic Games, before his parents moved him away from the field where his chapped lips were the first to meet yours. You want to live inside the innocence of your memories for a few days, but post-war Bosnia is a poor choice for this. You find a statue of Vucko with his face blown off, identified by letters carved into a sturdy marble base in front of the stadium complex you watched on television years ago, now a mound of cracked cement and tortured metal. Like most of the city. As you search fruitlessly for a place to spend the night, a former university student, living in the shelled-out remnants of a luxury hotel, asks, *Do you think the tourists will come back to us?*

You hitch a ride on the next departing aid truck headed for Croatia, where you can cross the Adriatic by ferry. You kissed plenty of Italian boys, too, and Venice is a safer place to indulge nostalgia. In Zagreb a woman you meet riding the streetcar offers you a room. As you walk with her up the cobblestone street, she points to a church riddled with bullet holes and says, *I call those the flowers of the war.* In Pula her words echo in your ears as you let the ferry leave without you.

You travel south slowly, hitching your way along the coast whenever the bus line leaves you stranded. Sometimes the roads are pitted with ditch-sized potholes, and as the drivers reverse directions, they warn you never to leave the shoulder. *What do you think made these holes?* they ask, but you don't know.

The military trucks and jeeps pass often, both UN troops and the Croatian army, willing or able or just crazy enough to pick their way through. They can't take on passengers, but they stop for a while, wait with you for the next NGO supply truck to come along. The local men give you pointers, islands off the coast to visit or avoid, places to spend the night, usually extra rooms you rent from hard-looking old ladies draped in black. Everyone is good to you. They share meals, refuse to take your kuna, and always, always, shake off questions about the war. *Look, this is beautiful country*, they say. *Tell your friends, what we once were, will be again.*

You believe them. You pass road crews working with shovels, rakes, and pickaxes, watch façades of buildings being painted when the bomb damage inside goes unrepaired. You ask a man with only one arm why he bothers painting a house with no roof. He shrugs, his pinned-up sleeve jerking to the rhythm of the roller. *The roof is beyond my help.* You watch him finish from a café table down the street, and three espressos later you twitch in your chair, partly from caffeine, mostly because you didn't offer to help.

You like riding in the supply trucks best. The main road hiccoughs along the coastal cliffs, and the seats are high enough to see the shoreline down below. The start-and-stop motion of the groaning diesel engine fuses with the hard slam of water against stone. In Dalmatia, Croatia's southern coast, land meets the Adriatic abruptly. The border between them is as violent as the recent history, like a splintered mountain range hammered into the sea. The islands, some too small to be inhabited, are lush tree-green tufts littering the blue expanse.

The shore is unpredictable. Dark, sharp rock cuts into the rubber soles of your tennis shoes. Sometimes you scramble over the rocks and follow an almost path to the waterline. The formations create natural pools where you splash around with turtles that snap at the air between you and then recede into their shells. Rock-colored frogs startle you with their croaks, and schools of small fish swim as one. You love the pristine wildness, the sea smell that is briny but not abused. Everywhere you stop, you search for other travelers. What you see is always yours to enjoy alone.

The road ends at Croatia's southernmost tip, at the walls of a fortress city built into the sea. Stari Grad, the old town, is protected by a shimmering white curtain of stone built in the thirteenth century. It reminds you of Camelot. Dubrovnik was bombed for eight straight months, calling attention to what was previously a brutal, unobtrusive war. In all your travels you have never seen a place more steeped in a fantasy past. You circle the wall and admire the town from a vantage twenty-five meters high. You poke around in towers, stand upon ramparts, and stare down as waves merge with the white stone. The steep-cut stairs, cobbled streets, tiled roofs, and marble squares create an atmosphere that fills your head with images of jousting knights lumbering down the *placa* atop armored horses. Your fantasies are all about rescue, although in real life you prefer to fix your own messes. By the time your stroll ends, Paris is your second favorite city.

Dubrovnik's sidewalk cafés are filled with modern-day knights: peacekeepers and health workers and soldiers of all nations. After six weeks alone, Dubrovnik is a hard place to feel lonely. You sip espresso with a few Doctors-Without-Borders on a weekend break from Tusla. The one from Bulgaria grasps your hands and says, *America. Great, great culture. John Wayne—bang bang, Pearl Jam, Las Vegas.* You search for somewhere to focus your grin and notice the columns across the street have three faces carved into the moldings on top. The central figure looks like Shakespeare. It's easy to drown out the background chatter of aid programs and reconstruction and simply believe this is an elaborate stage, a place designed to indulge anyone who wants to shrug off life for a while. The walls have already proven they can outlast any siege.

Outside the old town gate, the past greets you at a makeshift soccer field. Mijan is memory twice reflected. You know him from Mickey's, a bar back home where you flirted with him, a monosyllabic busboy, over the protests of your work friends. Not that it mattered. He ignored you then. He's still as round-cheeked as your lost boy, with full lips that you've never seen chapped. Mijan's eyes are green, not blue, but the eyelashes are the same, and so is the intensity of his game.

You sit on the sidelines and cheer until he scores the winning goal. You expect this and tell him so after the game. You ask, *Do you remember? Lina? From Mickey's? Part of the HBO crowd?*

He says, *Of course*, although it's clear he doesn't. He invites you along to a celebratory fish fry in the back of a friend's restaurant. Mijan's English is much improved, and he fires off questions about the bartenders and the regular bands as he teaches you to de-bone the whole fish you are served. *Best time of my life. Best bar in the city*, he repeats to you and the others, drinking to the prosperity of his adopted home and reunited friends. He is as anxious to get back to your country as you are content to stay put in his. You mistake this mutual enthusiasm for common ground.

You say goodbye to Fatima, the last in a line of widows with spare rooms, and stay with Mijan, who maintains the resort he helped rebuild. There are no guests, just a few locals enjoying the sundeck and the volleyball nets strung up along the beach. You watch every sunrise and sunset with Mijan, and the living is easy in between. After two months, the words *marriage* and *visa* finally register as more than playful teasing. The whole town thinks you'll be returning to New York together. You don't know how to tell him you've been planning your return even longer than he has. You think maybe he's the man to cure your ambivalence. The prospect of leaving Europe for love is appealing. Completing the circle would be a sort of progress.

Still, you try to distance yourself from Mijan and do some exploring on your own. Everywhere you walk, the locals stop and redirect you. *Mijan is playing soccer, go, go. Mijan is making pizza at Arturo's, hurry back now. Mijan borrowed his cousin's boat, meet him down by the dock behind the Pile gate.* You don't understand why he wants to leave this life in order to bus tables in the States. When you ask, he reminds you *How very American you can be.*

You slip out the gate and hop on a waiting bus before anyone corrals you. It's a local, and you like seeing where the real folks live. Within a half-hour you are in the suburbs of the city, driving past typical communist-era apartment complexes, ten-story green-gray boxes arranged in an H formation. The crippled buildings surprise you. The rubble is usually carefully swept and boarded over, but these pre-fab monstrosities aren't built to last. You respect the Croats even more for recognizing what's not worth saving.

The route ends at a high ridge above the shore. You file out with the other passengers, already peeking through the windows for a way to hike down. You spent the past few weeks watching Mijan play and are tired of being idle. You walk in the opposite direction from the others, and the bus driver begins to shout at you.

You wonder if Mijan has radioed around for you, and when this heavyset woman leaves her bus and sets out in your direction, you ignore her. You pick up the pace when you hear the heavy breathing behind you, but she tackles you at the waist and knocks you down. Your bag flies out ahead of you and explodes on impact, sending sharp rocks and pebbles over you both. You throw your arms up to protect yourself, and they are burned from the heat of the explosion, along with most of your hair. The bus driver's body covers most of yours, and her left leg is broken in three places.

At the hospital, you are given your own room and treated with extreme care. A fidgety man in a worn Italian suit confesses that no embassy or relief organization has been informed of your accident. You shrug, fall asleep, and wake up beloved for shielding them from bad publicity.

People visit as you mend, the conversations focused on better times ahead. Nobody ever blames you. A few merely ask, *How come you didn't listen when she warned you to stop?*

Mijan always answers, explaining that *Americans don't like to be told what to do.* He is ever-present in the folding chair closest to your bed, but he never mentions the future any more. On your last day you ask, *Why do you keep that minefield there?*

His eyes grow cold as his face heats up. *Because the war will come again. It always comes again.*

Third ᗫate

ᛕarim Malcolm was a creature of habit, and he was late. Tessa searched for him over the heads of middle-school children racing for home. A few students were her height or taller, mostly girls who blossomed prematurely. Tessa paid extra attention to these girls with women's bodies caught in the surge of attention they received from adolescent boys, and the men who impersonated them. She'd never understand why some of her most likeable colleagues turned perv in the presence of developing beauty. There was the occasional man-sized boy in her classroom, but this never sent her into uncontrollable spasms of lust. The man part, no matter how appealing, never eclipsed the boy inside. These girls weren't any less transparent, no matter how many half-clothed pop idols they tried to emulate.

Karim was different. Far above any man she had ever dated or known. In the teacher's breakroom last month, Karim said he valued experience over innocence because he preferred things that grew, rather than diminished, with time. That's when Tessa began to think of him as more than just an attractive colleague.

Tonight was their third date. Tessa shifted in the chunky heels that made the best of her calves (also chunky, no matter how many hours she put in at the gym). Not that Tessa had been to the gym recently. She led a healthy, active life and accepted that her body was designed to be round. Years of *Oprah* had taught her that much. Tessa turned thirty-nine last month, but she wasn't bothered. While she *had* lost some of her youthful firmness, she gained wisdom without becoming bitter or cynical. She believed that was worth two dress sizes. Any man who thought differently simply wasn't worth pursuing.

Karim was worth pursuing, even if her most comfortable heels made her feet ache after a full day on her feet. There were many teachers who could instruct from the comfort of their cushioned desk chairs, but Tessa wasn't one of them. She needed all her nervous energy to think. Karim worked from a lectern, standing perfectly still and composed in his British-butler way. The students called him Jeeves or Mr. Sul, which Tessa had feared was anti-Islamic until she learned it was only the abbreviation for "stiff upper lip." In Brooklyn, even post-9/11, being half-British and imitating his teachers from public school—which in England meant boarding school for some bizarre reason—was his more conspicuous heritage. Karim seemed a bit stuffy before you got to know him (his wardrobe was excessively fancy for a teacher), but that was just the sort of man he was. He thought details were important.

Karim was already forty, but he had the smoothest skin she'd ever seen on a man. It made her want to look her best for him. He reminded Tessa of her Aunt Angela, who maintained her appearance no matter what kind of family craziness was going on around her. It was a quality Tessa admired and tried to emulate as best she could. Style, like many other things, didn't come naturally to her. Tessa had to work hard for the things she wanted.

Karim supervised the main exit on release, but the courtyard was almost empty now. It wasn't like him to shirk his responsibilities, and Tessa's fingers went straight to her mouth before she remembered her manicure. She didn't want anything to interfere with their date for Thai food in Astoria. Karim had this secret restaurant treasure that Tessa knew all about because her cousin Enza had taken her there last year. Karim had laughed and said, "I keep forgetting you're a *real* New Yorker." Tessa still felt the residue of that compliment in her fingers and toes.

Sean barreled into her, and they each held on for balance. He was going through his first growth spurt and had lost his usual grace. "I told Cesar I'd help build sets for the play. Tell Nana for me?"

"That's not the rule," she said, but Sean was already running down the hall. Tessa stepped outside and saw her Aunt Donna near her usual spot on the bus bench across the street. She was already pacing. Tessa waved, but her aunt had her head down. Aunt Donna hugged herself, rocking and muttering as she walked. Her long hair was bone-in-the-desert white but wild from neglect. The man's overcoat she wore over layers to keep herself warm through the long day outdoors, and her mumbling—a litany of re-minders and warnings to stay vigilant and protect the boy—made her seem like a bag lady.

Aunt Donna was like her coat, a fine thing gone ragged from years of hard wear. Her two sons dead before they were men, a happy marriage turned bitter, then widowed and left to raise a baby after her granddaughter, sweet little Katie, passed.

Aunt Donna was eighty-two now, and she brought Sean to school every morning and then waited outside until it was time to take him home again. She spent her days on that bench in good weather or bad, and there was no illness or ache that could stop her vigilance. While Sean's mother had been fond of school, his grandmother had played hooky as early as third grade. She was keeping an eye on the school to prevent this and any other possi-ble dangers she had experienced with her own children or learned about from other mothers. Tessa had hoped she would stop once Sean was enrolled here, but she couldn't fault her aunt for choos-ing to protect her great-grandson the only way she knew how.

"Does she worry you?" Karim said, startling Tessa from behind. His hand pointed to Aunt Donna, who looked to be arguing with the newly planted tree.

"All the time," Tessa said with a sigh.

"Your insight is such a gift." He kissed the side of her head. His bangs brushed against her temple, and the unexpected contact made her shiver. "Hey, do you like Orson Welles?"

Tessa nodded automatically.

"*A Touch of Evil* is playing at the Moving Image at nine. Want to go?"

"I don't think I've seen that one." Tessa only knew he had something to do with that old *War of the Worlds* movie that caused some sort of crazy real-life panic.

"Great. Seven, at the restaurant?"

Tessa smiled through her disappointment, and he moved away as quickly as Sean. Karim wasn't from New York, so he knew how to drive and kept a car in the city. She hoped he would offer a lift to the restaurant. The third date was a threshold you passed through to become a real couple. It wasn't gentlemanly to make a woman take the subway alone at night. You met your *friends* in front of restaurants, but Tessa had learned a thing or two in the twenty-five years she'd been dating. Voicing those kind of expectations too early only hurried men off to their next relationship.

Tessa walked slowly toward her aunt. Karim was the kind of man that fit nicely with the life she had worked so hard to establish. Men like Karim didn't eat at the diner where she used to work, and that had been the extent of her dating pool. A romantic evening was a six-pack on the stoop and maybe some takeout Chinese as her date tried to talk his way upstairs for the night.

During their first date they talked over coffee so long they missed dinner. Then they trekked off to SoHo for Italian gelato from a place Karim had heard about from friends in TriBeCa. They chose the same flavor, a combination of chocolate and hazelnut, called *baci*, which meant *kiss*. He rode past his stop on the subway and walked her all the way to her door. His first kiss was a perfectly chaste goodnight, and the second, after a Moroccan meal served on the floor while they lounged on giant pillows, was more suggestive.

Aunt Donna paced the length of the bus bench, and both children and adults sidestepped her path. Tessa touched her aunt's arm to get her attention. Aunt Donna clutched her purse to her chest and cringed as if avoiding a punch.

"It's me." Tessa placed her own scarf around her aunt's face to warm her. "Sean's going to help his friend make the set for the school play next week. He'll probably be a couple of hours, okay?" "Extra credit?" Tessa nodded. Aunt Donna attended all the parent meetings. She knew extracurricular activities were important even in the early grades.

"Boy's inside. Safe. Good boy. College. I'll wait." Aunt Donna settled back onto the bench, and the anxious movement gradually left her.

Tessa's family had valued hard work over education and believed these two things were mutually exclusive. Men worked with their bodies, not their minds. Women were their bodies. Their work was marriage and motherhood—first you worked to find it, then you worked to hold it all together. Tessa absorbed these beliefs without question, but the old ways didn't work for her. The neighborhood no longer sustained working men, traditional stay-at-home moms, or large extended families fused together in mind and purpose. To survive as her family split apart and reformed, Tessa had to open herself up to new ways of thinking.

Tessa squeezed her aunt's shoulder, adjusted the scarf to protect her from the wind, and started walking home. Sometimes Tessa didn't blame her aunt for believing this was still a bad place to live. Most of the graffiti and garbage was gone, and so were the gangs, although sometimes you couldn't tell. The gangsta look was fashionable, down to faces fixed cold in that *I am prepared to hurt you* way. Tessa remembered the real thing too clearly to be confused. The mix of rage and despair she feared as a child was carried in the body. It wasn't a hard expression that made her walk faster even in daylight, but a body twitching out a Morse code of violence.

It was still a place with dark apartments in unremarkable brick buildings built for longshoremen and their families. The lifeless riverfront was hidden behind a chain-link fence topped with razor wire, and the only green in the neighborhood was near the sewage treatment plant that made any downwind breeze unwelcome, even in summer. It was, at best, only a scrubbed-up version of itself, popular now because the commute to Manhattan was short. It was still gritty, but not dangerous. Tessa noticed the newcomers loved the neighborhood not only for its convenience, but for its *flavor*.

Tessa enjoyed the amenities that followed her new neighbors across the bridge. She loved samosas and sushi as much as she loved pizza and pierogies, and she stopped off at the natural-foods store for seedy seven-grain bread almost as often as she stopped for semolina at the Italian deli or pumpernickel at the Polish bakery. Tessa was lucky that her parents had bought a house, because rents now were usually quadruple the mortgage payment Tessa made to the bank each month. Many of the families who had lived in the neighborhood for three or more generations, doing their best to weather through the hard times, like her own, had been forced to move.

Her house was squeezed into a narrow space between two large apartment buildings, and steep metal steps led to the entrance on the middle of three floors. Tessa's parents had bought a *fixer-upper*, then discovered that neither one of them was particularly good with do-it-yourself home repair. The house had chugged through the years with its smoky, inefficient boiler, garbled wiring, and warped, drafty windows. Last year, to celebrate her graduation and her new job, she dipped into her home equity and splurged on a renovation. Tessa had knocked out the walls on the main level, creating one large open area divided only by the L-shaped kitchen countertop, and the three-paneled window in front flooded the whole floor with light. Tessa wasn't savvy about home décor, but her mother had made elaborate plans over the years, waiting on Lotto winnings to set everything in motion. Her mother's windfall had never materialized, but Tessa had absorbed her ideas without ever paying them much attention.

Karim was impressed that she owned property in the city, and she could imagine him standing by her side at the mortgage-burning party she would throw in just five short years. Tessa was anxious for Karim to meet her family, especially her mother. Even though the deed was now in Tessa's name only, Rose Anna deserved to light the match even if she was raising hell in Tampa instead of Brooklyn. Karim would love her family. Enza made tons of money with computers, Lina was a world traveler, and Nikki had seven kids but never looked frazzled or frumpy.

When Tessa reached home, she went straight to her desk and signed on to the Internet so she could read about Orson Welles before her date. With Karim, you didn't just watch a movie, you thought about it afterwards. How it was made, what it meant, how the actors performed their roles. Directors were important, too. Tessa hadn't known many people who thought about a movie as anything more than entertainment, but she liked how thinking about all these things made her feel, like she had to pay real close attention to every little thing around her or she might miss out.

While Tessa hadn't grown up in an intellectual environment or attended fancy schools, she learned gads of information about Orson Welles from just a few clicks. He was an actor, director, announcer (the panic was from a *radio* broadcast), and writer. It didn't take long for Tessa to feel ashamed that she knew so little about him to begin with. It was one more reason she was happy to spend time with Karim.

The phone rang as soon as Tessa disconnected the modem. "Hello?"

"Tessa, you have to come right now." Sean's voice ranged from soprano to bass. Puberty was advancing on him daily. "We're in big trouble."

"What's wrong?" Sean wasn't an excitable child. "Did you break something?"

"Jeeves has Nana in his office. He's got her all scared and confused. It's bad."

"I'll be right there." Tessa ran, jogged, then power-walked the ten blocks to school. She made her way up the steps and corralled Sean by his sleeve without breaking stride. She slipped past the guard who flirted with her daily, then entered Karim's office without knocking. Aunt Donna was squeezed between the school's two other guards. She was rocking and praying the rosary, a nervous habit that had outlasted her faith. "What are you doing to my aunt?"

"Tessa?" His voice had a surprised, breathy quality that shifted her thoughts briefly back to romance. "We discussed this earlier."

"Discussed what?" Tessa advanced on him, crowding his space. "Terrifying the elderly?" Tessa turned from him before he could answer and kneeled at her aunt's side. She didn't appear to know Tessa was in the room with her. "It's okay, I'm here. Everything's okay. Sean, talk to your Nana." Sean squeezed between his Nana and the guard, and she put her arm around him, forcing him to rock with her on the couch.

"She's related to you?" Karim asked, as if he couldn't fathom such a thing.

"She lives with me. Sean lives with me. If you'd ever bothered to pick me up at my house, you might know that." Tessa could hear Dr. Phil chiding in her head.

Karim walked to his desk, picked up some paperwork, then put it down again. "But…I asked you about her this afternoon."

Tessa waved her arms. "Of course I worry about my aunt!"

Karim stepped back. On their first date, they had bonded over the aggressiveness of Italian hand gestures. He had been traumatized by an overly emphatic semester spent at the University of Perugia, and Tessa, the timid child in a boisterous family, understood his pain. "We miscommunicated."

Miscommunicated. In this moment, Tessa could understand why so many students couldn't relate to him. "Why would you do this without consulting Principal LoBello? Dom's known my aunt since her children were students at P.S. 34. He knows who she was, what she's been through." Tessa charged into his space again, and Karim took equal steps back.

"Sean's a great kid. I wanted to make sure he was getting what he needed to stay that way."

"Why didn't you ask me about him then?" Tessa put her hand

on his arm, wanting to rein in her anger and bridge the gap between them. "I grew up here. I know these kids, their families. Do
you think Sean's the only child in this community being raised by
a grandmother?" Karim stared down at his arm, and Tessa felt the
pressure of her grip. She let go, shaking out her fingers.

Karim massaged his forearm. "I don't think of potential
abuse as a community concern. My first priority is to protect
my students."

Tessa squeezed her fists to keep still. "Abuse is a community
concern!"

Gloria, the female guard, stood up. "I told him she never
caused no harm. She's a little wrong in the head, but half Brooklyn
be in jail if that was a crime." Karim gestured for her to leave, and
the other guard quickly followed her out.

Karim cleared his throat once, then twice more. "She was agi-
tated and resistant. I called Social Services."

Tessa closed her eyes for a minute, trying to imagine herself
home where she belonged, in the bath preparing for their date.
"They have a caseworker, a woman they've dealt with for years.
I'll call now."

"It's taken care of," she told Karim, after she'd reached her.
"Sean, wait for me outside. We'll walk together." He stood up, and
Aunt Donna followed, her arm protectively around him. Tessa
turned her attention back to Karim. "Are we having dinner?" Her
voice was so sharp it seemed like she was channeling her mother.
This pleased Tessa. Rose Anna, for all her flaws, had always protected her family.

"We did make plans," Karim said blandly.

"Then I'll see you *at the restaurant*." Dr. Phil be damned.

Tessa walked down the school steps, and Sean jumped off the
bench to meet her. "He's a dried-out turd! I don't know why you
like him."

Tessa couldn't help but laugh. "Do you really want to butt into
my dating life just months before your thirteenth birthday?"

Aunt Donna was sitting on the bus bench, still mouthing

prayers she no longer believed in. It was a nervous habit she denied and both Tessa and Sean ignored. Tessa took her aunt's hand and said, "My mother called when you were out. Let's get going so you can call her back."

As soon as they reached home, Tessa called in reinforcements. Her Aunt Angela arrived by cab from Park Slope within a half-hour, and Nikki followed a few minutes later with her two youngest children. Nikki got the children settled doing homework and moved on to making dinner. Aunt Angela set up her cell with speakerphone (always the newest and best), then hurried Tessa out of the room so the sisters could talk freely. Tessa could hear her mother's voice booming through the speaker, comforting her aunt, as she prepared for her date. The noise grew progressively louder as Nikki searched through the cabinets for the right pots and pans, the children finished their homework and argued over video games, and Aunt Donna talked and laughed amid the familiar chaos. Tessa, who had grown comfortable with quiet, didn't want to leave her house when it seemed so full of life.

She sat across from Aunt Angela and said, "I think maybe I should cancel on Karim."

"Dump Jeeves," Sean called out, his eyes fixed on his game. "Yeah!" Tessa wasn't sure if the yeah was meant for her or the on-screen action.

"Don't you dare!" Aunt Angela said. She smoothed out her hair and her skirt, as if she expected Karim to walk in at any moment. "Go enjoy yourself. I don't want you ending up like me."

"You didn't do too badly in the end." Aunt Angela, after a life spent caring for others, had married a man she'd worked with for thirty years.

"Cancel," Nikki called from the kitchen. Tessa knew the fridge was understocked, but whatever Nikki had scraped together smelled better than any carefully crafted meal Tessa had ever cooked. "When you draw things out, it takes them longer to disappoint you."

"Mom, you're damaging my psyche *again*," reported Nikki's fifteen-year-old daughter.

"Preparing, not damaging, my darling," Nikki replied.

Tessa waited for Aunt Donna to chime in, but she was dozing on the couch. Aunt Angela took Tessa by her shoulders and escorted her to the door. "Go. We'll all wait up. Bring back dessert if you can."

Tessa had to switch subway lines to get to the restaurant, and the wait for the second train was a long one. The first to arrive had a rush-hour crush, and Tessa let that one go. The next was no better, and Tessa glanced at her watch and pushed her way on with a sigh. She believed cabs were an extravagance, financially and environmentally, except for reasons of late-night safety. A short man wedged next to her was eye deep in the low-cut dress she had worn, and Tessa blamed this on Karim's appalling lack of consideration.

Tessa's heels pounded the sidewalk between the subway and the restaurant, although she tried to regulate her temper through deep breathing. She didn't want to ruin the relationship she'd been waiting her grown-up life to have over one misunderstanding and a subway lech. Her heels began to show some mercy, until she saw his BMW parked steps from the restaurant.

Inside, Karim was sipping a Thai iced tea and munching on a curry puff. "You started without me?" she asked, as he rose to greet her.

"You're really late," he said, showing his watch.

Tessa sat down, and picked up the menu to hide her face. She needed water to cool the rushing heat. "The N took forever to come."

"You took the subway?" For the second time today, he questioned her as if he couldn't fathom such a thing.

"You know I don't drive." Her words were clipped, her habit when students stretched the limits of her patience. "How else would I get here?"

"I should have offered to pick you up." Karim moved his napkin from his lap to the table, then back to his lap. "That was thought-less. I apologize."

One of the twin owners arrived with the wine Karim had se-lected, and Tessa's mood eased by the glass. "Why didn't you tell me about your aunt?" he asked, after they had ordered.

Tessa shrugged. "People talk. I assumed you knew."

Karim drummed his fingers against the table, showing a ner-vousness she'd never seen before. "I didn't. The gossip mongers don't exactly seek me out."

"But you see Sean and me together all the time."

It was his turn to shrug. "You're very…chummy with the stu-dents."

"Too chummy?" she asked.

"Not at all," he said. "I admire how easily you get along."

"Thank you." Tessa's neck had been tight all afternoon but was finally loosening. A second order of appetizers arrived at the table, and Tessa speared a curry puff. "Tell me about *your* family."

"Not much to tell," he said. "I'm a second-generation only child."

"Both your parents were only children?" Tessa's nose crinkled as she tried to fathom a world without siblings, cousins, or aunts.

"My mother had family in Kabul, but they literally consider her dead. Rebellious daughters don't get much love there."

"Rebellion didn't go over too well in my family either," Tessa said with a smile. "But your mom must miss them?"

Karim shook the idea off. "My mother hated the restrictions placed on women in even a moderate Muslim family. She never looked back."

"I grew up in an apartment building where everyone was related to me through my mother." Tessa's hands flew out auto-matically before she drew them back. "I prayed for rescue, but you wouldn't believe how much I miss them now."

Tessa eyed the last dumpling, and Karim served it to her with a deft flick of his chopsticks. "You can't miss what you've never had. I loved being the center of my parents' world. Still do."

Tessa considered being the focus of all her mother's attention, then refilled her wine glass to the brim.

"So, did your aunt raise you, too?"

"My mother went to Florida to help my sister-in-law through a bad pregnancy, and then she stayed on after the baby was born." Tessa went back to her wineglass, although it was time to switch to water. "My brother Vinny reconciled with his wife at his daughter's high-school graduation. They have two children twenty years apart."

"Sweet," Karim said. "And your aunt?"

Tessa shrugged. "I had the house, and she needed help with Sean."

"That's a lot of responsibility to take on alone."

"That's the point," Tessa said. "With family you don't have to be alone."

"But, what happens when…" As Karim's voice trailed off, the condiments captured his interest.

"That choice would be up to Sean." Tessa took the fish-sauce bottle from his hand and placed it in the corner where it belonged. "His father's alive. He was messed up a long time, but he's getting his PhD now. Sean spent last summer with him in Colorado."

"PhD?"

"He wasn't a neighborhood boy," Tessa said.

"So, Sean might eventually go live with his father."

"Only if he wanted to. You said yourself he's a great kid."

"He really is, Tessa." Karim loosened his tie, as close to casual as she had ever seen him. "You and your aunt should be proud."

"We are."

Their entrees arrived, and they shared them as agreed. Karim's pan-seared whole fish was exquisite and made her choice of green-curry chicken seem mundane. She liked the idea of their relationship unfolding over a series of delicious, carefully chosen meals. "Karim, can I ask you a question?"

"You may."

"We've had some great conversations," she started. "Wonderful. But I feel like I don't know very much about you."

Tessa waited as Karim chewed slowly. "We talk endlessly," he said when he was done.

Tessa took a bite of the fish to compose herself. The chile was subtle, with a cumulative kick. "We talk about school, movies, and New York, but I've never seen where you live, or who you live with."

"I live alone."

"You could have a roommate, and I wouldn't know."

"I couldn't possibly have a roommate." His arms crossed as if she'd accused him of something terrible.

"Why not?"

"Because I'm an only child," he said. "I've never learned to share."

Tessa drained her glass for courage. "I'm just saying I think it's a little odd that I haven't been to your place, and you haven't been to mine."

"Are you inviting yourself home with me?" he asked. "On a school night?"

Tessa wasn't sure if he was teasing her, and she blamed this on the wine. She picked up the glass of water she'd been neglecting, and one of the twins immediately refilled it for her.

"I like how slow we're taking things." Tessa waited for him to answer, but he focused upon the last few morsels on his plate. "But I want to know you better."

"I live more inside my head than you do," Karim said, after the plates were cleared and they had both passed on dessert. "To me, talking about ideas is very intimate."

"I'll try to remember that," Tessa said.

She was dissatisfied with his answer without knowing why. This must have showed, because he said, "I admire how connected you are to the world, how rooted in the everyday. You believe so strongly in people and connections. I could learn from you in that regard."

"Would you really like to?" She liked that she had something to offer him. She believed it was true.

"Yes. Of course," he said, as he stood. "Shall we move on to the film?"

"Why don't you come meet my family instead?" She smoothed out the wrinkles in her dress. "I feel so good right now, I think I'd be too restless for a movie."

"What about the film?" He held the door for her. It was a little thing, but it moved her. Almost enough to sit through the movie for him.

"My aunt has company right now. Her mind is so much clearer when her family's all around her. We could drive down to Juniors and get cheesecake for dessert. Do you know Juniors? It's a Brooklyn institution, something no New Yorker should miss."

Karim lifted his shoulders and let them fall. "But it's a one-time showing."

"My family doesn't get together very often," she countered.

"You're waving your hands around again."

Tessa stepped back. "I didn't mean to bring back the trauma."

"Now you're making fun of me," he said, his hands tucked silently behind him.

"A little," she said. She wanted him to let go, agree to have some messy human fun. She leaned forward, displaying her dress to full advantage. "Don't you like it?"

"I like you." He leaned in, and she expected him to kiss her. "But I was looking forward to this. Welles takes this mystery piece he was forced to direct and elevates it beyond the cliché plot."

Tessa rocked on her heels. "Is it available on DVD?"

"I don't know." He shrugged, grudgingly. "Possibly."

"We could watch it together tomorrow. I really would like to see it with you. We could get some wine and some food, and go to your place. Or mine, if you don't have television or a player." Tessa leaned in to him again. She wanted to win this, and she didn't care how. "Doesn't that sound nice?"

"Tessa…"

She tugged him closer by his lapels. "They're all *real* New Yorkers."

He drew her hands from his coat, and she thought she'd won

him over. "Tessa, it's way too soon for that sort of thing between us." He let her hands fall to her side.

She moved away and focused her attention on the sickly tree by the curb. Karim came up behind her and pulled her close. She leaned into him, and he still felt so solid and so right. "We have to leave now, or we'll miss the beginning." He let her go, and she was sorry. She wished he could have held her a while longer.

"You go on to the movie," she said.

"You're not coming?" He tilted his head, as if he finally realized she was moving out of focus.

"It's just not for me," she said, before her voice began to crack. She wanted to say more, but that was all that really mattered.

Reunion

Franca's father lumbered out of the taxi, swatted the arm she offered, and took quick, short steps that made her wince. He buckled into the stoop's middle step, the force of bones on brick breaking his habitual stoicism. He used to make the fire escape tremble, an ox of a man in constant motion. Now his flesh was a suit several sizes too large. "I want to go home, *carissima*."

"You're almost there, Pop."

Franca scanned the block for her husband's truck, a black F-150 with *Jack is all you need to know about home repair!* running along both sides. He had announced this slogan at the party Franca threw after his small-business loan was approved. He held up a LaGuardia College catalog and said, "Now that I know I'm a creative genius, I'll just work my way through school with this hard- labor crap." The abundance of shoulder pats Franca received that evening revealed just how many friends remembered her best friend Lina coining that catchphrase for him during career week in junior high.

Her father pressed his hand to his chest, then tried to disguise the pain as a tickle in his throat. Franca wiggled her cell, so he believed she had a plan. "Tessa said she'd be home in case Jack got held up. We'll take the stairs real slow."

"*Voglio il mio paese.* I don't want to die here."

Jack had warned her to wait for the private ambulance, but they had been hours behind schedule, and the hospital needed to flip the bed or charge them another night. Now she wasn't sure how she'd get her father upstairs without Jack's help. "This was your home for forty years. I need you to be patient a little while longer."

"*Ma dai*, this was never my home."

Franca squeezed her eyes shut until she had them under control. She would not sully his day with tears. She cupped her father's chin. "I thought I was your home."

He took her hand and kissed it, princess style, a habit that had outlived her childhood. "*Hai ragione*. But my last steps must be on the *lungomare*, facing the sea."

"I'm trying, Pop." Franca sat and rested her head on his shoulder, and it felt like touching a stranger. She never thought of a shoulder, mostly bone, as something that could shrivel. "Flying is more difficult now. All sorts of rules that keep changing, and I want to make sure I get it right for you."

The Hatzolah ambulance turned the corner, and Franca stood to flag them down, thinking maybe they could find her the help she needed. They pulled up, and Tessa waved from the passenger seat. Her cousin had more energy now than she did as a child, something Franca found hard not to envy. "Fat Louie's dispatching at the car service. He gave me a call," Tessa said.

Tessa hugged Franca, then kissed her uncle's head. "We're going to get you comfy, Uncle Mass. Don't worry."

One medic set her father up with oxygen as the other two unloaded the equipment. "What do you know?" Franca asked.

Tessa looked down at her own heels, which were tapping. A giveaway to anyone who knew her well.

"Spill," Franca commanded.

"You have enough to deal with right now." Tessa tugged at her lip, a gesture that belonged on her mother, Rose Anna, and Franca's oldest ache palpated. She couldn't remember her own mother, and Franca thought of her father more in terms of how he was different, the old world versus the new.

"I can tell you know where Jack is," Franca said.

"Fat Louie saw Jack at the Polish bar," Tessa said. "When he got your call from the hospital, he knew Jack wasn't in any shape to help. He offered to pull some drivers if we needed them. He said Uncle Mass never made him any money, but he was always a classy guy."

Tessa thrust out her chest, licked her thumb, and counted an imaginary bankroll Fat Louie-style. Franca bit back her smile. Their childhood was colorful enough the first time through. "And the rescue crew?"

Tessa rocked on her heels. "Customers from my diner days."

The men whisked her father upstairs in a canvas chair with poles and rubber hand grips. When her father refused to get into the hospital bed she'd set up in her living room, Tessa sent the men up two more flights for his favorite chair, a recliner Franca had asked Jack to bring down from the apartment last night. When her Dad was settled in his chair, watching a DVD of Turandot performed at the Met with his fancy, noise-free headphones, Franca handed off the last of Jack's beers to the crew. When they were done, they left behind the canvas chair.

Franca put her chin on the kitchen table. "I can't even get into the Italian consulate. It's like waiting in line for Springsteen tickets. Now that he's out, I'm going to have to get up in the middle of the night and wait outside, then get someone to bring Pop over when it's time to open."

"I can take a day off. Just name the day, and I'll schedule something easy for the sub."

"They don't care he's sick. He's just a type, the homesick native. They'll break his heart if he catches on."

"Lina works with governments now," Tessa said.

"She hates me," Franca's stomach still fluttered when she thought of Lina.

"No." Tessa shrugged. "We're not in her thoughts much."

It was Franca's turn to look at the floor. "She made me her maid of honor, and I didn't even invite her to my wedding."

"She hasn't come back once," Tessa said.

"Did we ever give her a reason?"

Tessa stroked Franca's hair. "She's not in exile. Her *happy* just looked different than ours."

Franca asked, "You think she's happy?"

Tessa lifted her hands, palms up, as if weighing the possibilities. "She left and stayed gone."

Jack was at the door, his hands too unsteady to fit the key smoothly in the lock. Tessa said, "He drives that huge truck." She shivered as they listened to metal scratching metal.

The door finally jerked open. Jack grunted at her father on his way to the fridge. It was hard not to smile when he tossed the plastic ring in the trash. Franca said, "Some lovely men helped me out today. Couldn't send them home thirsty."

He leaned into the table, standing over Tessa and her signature v-neck. "Looking good, as always."

Franca snorted, years past jealousy. Tessa stood, and she was Jack's height in her platform maryjanes. "She needs you now, dumbass." Tessa rapped her knuckles against Jack's skull, another ferocious gift from her mother. "Get your head straight." She hugged the breath from Franca as she slid something into her back pocket. "That's her email. Reach out."

Jack said, "I hate your whole busybody family," as the clack of Tessa's heels receded.

Bile rose in her throat, but Franca checked on her father. He had drifted off, wheezing only slightly through his oxygen mask, a satisfied smile on his face. Puccini was his cure-all.

Jack plucked the big knife from the dish rack. "You'd run me through to save him."

She couldn't help but nod, yet her fingers twitched toward him. Franca missed the purity of what she felt before the drone of marriage set in. Lina was smart to run.

✸

Lina,

My father is dying. Please forgive my bluntness, but

I don't think I have time for all the things I ought to say to you. He wants to go home. Italy home, and how can I refuse him? He's from a small fishing village, Camogli, near Genoa (remember how he used salami as bait that time he took us fishing?). Nobody at the embassy will help me, and there's so much paperwork involved. They make me repeat my Italian, and then answer in slow English like I'm obviously stupid in any language. I call and call, but nothing ever gets resolved. If you can help me, I've never needed it more.

There was a time when I couldn't imagine twenty-four hours without you in them. It still seems strange that this is no longer true.

Would you believe me if I signed "love?" I do.

Franca

❋

Jack tore into the apartment, upsetting piles Franca had organized for her sleepover outside the embassy. "You knew she wasn't going to let me have my kids."

"That's not the version I heard." Franca was frying up five pounds of chicken breast on three burners, while marinara simmered on the fourth. Jack's ex worked full-time in retail, so Franca was Johnny and Sara's only respite from the processed crap their mother served daily. She pointed to the casserole dish covered in tinfoil. "I made the baked ziti with chicken and spinach they like. If they're not coming here, you need to take it over there while it's still hot."

Jack opened the fridge, but Franca was done stocking beer. "Maria screws with me again, and you don't give a shit?"

"I don't think a sobriety chip's too much for a mother to expect."

Jack slammed the fridge, making the hinges bleat. "You think she's a lousy fucking mom, and I don't drink any more than anyone around here."

"You don't drink any less, either."

"I'm their *fa·ther*!" He rested between the two syllables, as if speaking the word was exhausting.

"Then make sure they get the two fridges worth of food I've been making for them. I'll have everything sorted and organized, with directions, before I leave."

"This is your damn fault." Jack kicked the table leg, threatening a full day's work, and she plucked the frying pan from the rack and cocked it at him. Six years of kindness hadn't cured him.

"There's a meeting at the church. Go. You'll be happier when the kids are here."

Jack paced the table, switching directions with a speed that made her look away. "Why won't you stay?"

"Collect a few chips while I'm gone, and maybe I'll want to come back."

He yanked the pan from her in one swift motion and let it drop to the floor. "I am your husband."

"*I'm their father. I'm your husband,*" Franca mimicked. "Don't you get tired of swinging titles around?"

Jack kicked the door as he left, barking his frustration on the stairs. Her father emerged from the bathroom, slowly making his way to the door, which he closed, trailing his oxygen tank back to his chair. He was walking and breathing better now that he was home. "I didn't raise you to be cruel," he said softly.

The tears came hot and thick, bloated by shame. He placed his hand on her head. "You'll have some insurance money, and I want you to enjoy life some."

"I won't really be in a party mood, Pop."

"*Basta cosi.* I'm an old man, and you'll be in the country that invented love."

"I love those kids like they were mine." Her father joined in her sigh for Jack's son and daughter. They didn't deserve damaged, warring parents.

"You've been a good girl all your life. There's more out there for you. *Meglio.*"

"In *Italia*?"

"*Certo!*"

Franca laughed, despite herself. "I'm expecting that clean Mediterranean air you go on about to restore you completely."

"We'll see." For the moment, it was enough to see his broad-cheeked smile return.

❀

Lina,

Are you out there? Did my previous message get gobbled by your spam filter? I can't believe you'd ignore me. Are you angry that I married him? That I didn't even write to explain? God, I'd rather hear how much you hate me than wonder like this. My Dad seems to be doing better away from the hospital, but every day he asks me when we're going home. Does Europe feel like home to you? Has Italy ever tugged at you, or Poland, I guess, for your Dad?

Please write me.

Please.

❀

Franca had to let another person pass her in line. Cell phone usage wasn't allowed inside the embassy, and Tessa and her father were more than an hour late. She walked up to the guard again. "*Allora, mi lascia fuori per cinque minuti, per favore.*"

The guard removed his wrap-around sunglasses. "Lady, do I seem Italian to you?"

Not anymore. His eye-talian would have made her father shiver. "You didn't answer my English."

He showed her his profile. "You don't recognize a taciturn *black* man when you see one?"

Franca lifted her shoulders slightly. "Actually, you're more the color of a perfect cappuccino, and what's more Italian than that?"

He fought his smile hard, but he opened the door for her. "Born here. Born there. Y'all are crazy."

One of Fat Louie's cabs was waiting by the curb. Her fingers buzzed. She wanted this trip to happen, to have this time with her father.

"Franca."

She turned, and there was Nikki sitting on the steps, her fists slapping her thighs. Franca had spent her entire childhood watching Lina, her sister, worry exactly the same way. "The hospital?"

Nikki stood and shook her head slowly. Franca swayed into her arms. "Tessa said it was peaceful. He's at peace, sitting in the grand temple of opera, being serenaded by Puccini himself."

Franca could picture her father's personal Heaven, the Camogli seascape in the background. Nikki guided her into the taxi, and then Jack and his two children were waiting on the stoop when she reached home. As Nikki opened the door, Franca put her hand on her arm and asked, "Why would Lina ignore me now?"

❀

His urn was the new epicenter of her life. Sitting or standing, alone or in a group. Her eyes found it, no matter how many obstacles stood in the way. It wasn't fancy in the traditional way. No precious metals. No elaborate shapes or carvings. No jewels or saints. It was made of biodegradable recycled paper, elegant in the way of wedding invitations. It was shaped like a business portfolio and designed for transport. She chose it before the consulate informed her that ashes could be transported for interment only, from one mortuary directly to another. Her plan to scatter his ashes somewhere in his beloved Camogli was *vietato*. Forbidden. She had failed her father utterly.

Sara, Jack's earnest tween, squeezed her hand and whispered, "I loved him more than both my grandpas." Franca squeezed back, before Jack guided her to the couch. He seemed to believe grief resided in the legs.

He sat beside her, stroking the length of her arm. She sought the urn yet again, to curb her irritation. "I'll go to the meetings. We can afford a house now, and Maria won't fight full custody. She knows you're a better mom, she just needs an excuse like this to save face."

Franca shrugged herself free from him. Nikki walked in, her ear to her flip-top phone, and beckoned Franca. She pressed the phone into Franca's palm and brought it to her ear.

"Franca?"

"Lina?" Nikki quickly guided her into the bedroom for privacy. She pulled a packet of tissues from her purse and handed them to Franca, then placed some sort of fabric on the bed before she left.

"If you don't stop crying, I'll start." Franca could hear the rasp in her old friend's throat. "I didn't get your messages until Nikki called and I went hunting for them. I'm in Belgium now, and that was my Portugal account, which I've sort of been avoiding for romantic reasons. I'm so sorry about your dad."

Franca tried to collect herself. It was Lina's voice in speed and inflection, yet she sounded so foreign, as if she had never even been *born* in Brooklyn. "I feel like I've missed you every day you've been gone."

It was Lina's turn to fall apart. "Do people even know you're American?" Franca asked, to fill the air.

"Oh, they know," Lina said, and her laugh was still the same. Loud and unapologetic. "I know this is a bad time, but have you been happy?"

Franca drew a few breaths before she answered. "Not for a long while."

"Take a look at what Nikki left for you." The fabric was crescent shaped and dual-sided, purple fleece on the outside, lavender satin inside. It was only partly sewn together. "What is this?"

"First, you have to understand the golden rule of Italy: it is always better to seek forgiveness than to ask permission."

"I'm not breaking any rules that will get me into trouble." Two minutes, and Franca's hair was already in her mouth, a habit she had long outgrown.

"That's your American side talking. In Italy, the rules *cause* the trouble. Fly into Venice. I have a friend there who is very well connected."

Franca flipped the crescent over, then inside out. She shrugged, as if Lina could see her. "I don't get what this is for."

"It's a travel pillow, sweetie. Your father deserves to come home."

"You're suggesting—"

"Nikki will make it look perfect."

"It's not Nikki's sewing skills that worry me!"

"I need you to trust that I know what I'm doing, that even though it's been a really long time, I remember what your father means to you."

Franca shook her head. Absolutely not. Lina had always been in trouble, and obviously that hadn't changed. When Franca said, "La Fenice is in Venice," she was more surprised than Lina.

"You *are* your father's daughter."

"You'll meet my flight?" Franca asked, but it wasn't really a question anymore. She had spent her childhood watching Lina get out of trouble as easily as she got into it. Franca would take the risk. She would bring her father home.

A native of New York City, Valerie Fioravanti now lives in Sacramento, California, where she directs the Stories on Stage reading series, and teaches for the UCLA Writers' Extension. She has held a Fulbright fellowship to Italy and holds degrees from New Mexico State University in Las Cruces, and the New School in New York City. Her work has appeared in such publications as *North American Review, Cimarron Review,* and *Hunger Mountain. Garbage Night at the Opera,* the title story of which received a special mention in *Pushart Prize XXVIII,* is her first book.